The Lazy Postman

Jason Vikse

Joan,
Thanks for hosting book club!.
such a fun
Hope this story lives up
to the hype.

ISBN: 1467941832
ISBN 13: 978-1467941839

To Krista

Monday, August 18

The first thing I noticed was the mirrors.

The sun's reflection shone right into my eyes as I walked through the gate with my suitcases, its rays bouncing brightly off of a variety of unframed mirrors lying face-up on the ground to my left. I veered right, threw up my arm to shield my eyes, and felt a large hand grab my wrist.

"You might want to watch where you're swinging that kit of yours, son. You only get one chance to make a first impression."

I looked away from the mirrors and into a gruff, masculine face that matched the voice, wrinkle for wrinkle. Lines and spots, the medals of age, decorated the face; an advancing army that had claimed the top of his head and his arm, all the way up to my wrist. Age hadn't weakened his grip, but I imagined a smile hiding behind his eyes. A good thing too, because there wasn't one anywhere else.

"Sorry sir." I gulped. "It was the mirrors."

"You almost stepped on Patton."

I looked down. Centimetres away from my right foot lay a pug. A very fat, very old pug. It was sprawled out with all four legs pointing in different directions, like a wrinkly little compass. Patton opened one eye, flicked it up at me, and gave a soft snort. His meaning was clear. I was on probation.

The old man's voice interrupted the interspecies scolding. "Well?"

"It won't happen again, sir."

"Well, alright then. See that it doesn't." He stepped back and gave me the once-over. "Name's Noah. Like the ark. But I've only got one animal, and I hate rainbows. I'm the complex manager. Are you 2B?"

This was the first time since Lit 12 that Shakespeare had made any sense to me. 2B or not 2B? Was there still a chance at escaping? The only possible answer broke through my reluctance. Nope. Dad had already paid for two weeks rent. This was my new digs. "I'm 2B. Jordan Melville."

"Thought so. From Edmonton, right? Welcome to Victoria. Your father came by a few weeks ago. Thought the place was just what you needed, he said. Hope you don't want help with your luggage." With that, he dropped my arm, luggage and all, and turned away. My suitcase slipped out of my circulation-free hand and thumped to the floor directly in front of Patton. Patton blinked. I rubbed my wrist and followed Noah into the complex. I could hear the words my dad had said to me when he dropped me off at the curb just moments before.

"Welcome to life son. It's all about the people." Then he'd kicked me out of the car, and driven off, laughing. My dad has kind of a weird sense of humour.

I slipped the deadbolt and dropped my suitcases next to the hall closet. Noah had just given me the grand tour of the complex, which mostly consisted of me standing in the middle of the courtyard next to an empty and long-dry fountain, and turning in a slow circle while he pointed out all the wonderful features and amenities that Stony Creek Estates had to offer. I thought the name was a strange choice, since nowhere in sight was there a creek, stony or otherwise.

The complex was exactly how my dad had described it to me. Nine small units, arranged in a long rectangle with the entrance at the bottom end, four units up each side, and one at the top. Each unit had a small yard area in front, except for the first unit on the left, where the lawn had been replaced by mirrors. Noah had explained that the lawns had been put in as a way for the inhabitants to personalize their homes, which were otherwise carbon copies of each other; built in the 1960s.

Whether by conscious choice or apathetic avoidance, every resident had taken advantage of Noah's creative allowance. 2A, next to the house of mirrors, had a perfectly manicured front lawn that was entirely impersonal. Well-trimmed grass covered the entire space. Not a plant or a garden gnome in sight.

Next to that was the patch of dirt surrounding a long-dead rosebush, belonging to 3A. 4A had a Zen garden. A carefully positioned rock floated on a peacefully raked bed of sand. 5A was the unit on the end. It boasted a mixture of grass, perennials, dandelions, and at least two kinds of ivy which had climbed out of an old wooden flowerbox and seemed to be racing each other to the roof.

On the other side of the courtyard were four more units. The B side. At the far end 4B's entire lawn space was given over to a gigantic, historic barbeque. The windows were boarded over and Noah had commented that the unit was vacant so he'd had the BBQ installed for communal use. That was in 1974. It hadn't been used since.

3B was apparently inhabited by a collector of wind chimes and lawn ornaments. Cute plaster bunnies frolicked in the shadow of a faded plastic fawn, with thinly-leashed butterflies dancing in the breeze overhead.

Then came 2B and 1B. Me and Noah. And Patton. Both units had concrete patios poured in front of their doors, with cheap white patio chairs for absorbing any hours of leisure. Beside Noah's chair was a filthy metal water dish with a large brass "P" soldered to the side. My chair was heaped with what I'd assumed was the previous tenant's mail. Noah had pushed me towards it with a final gruff welcome.

"If you need anything, let me know. I'm always around." His face had puffed up with pride. "Haven't been away more than a day since I bought the place, save for that two-week Caribbean cruise I won back in 1982."

Noah had shaken my hand, which played havoc with my pins and needles, and pointed me towards my door.

Standing inside my new home away from home for the first time, I wondered what I'd gotten myself into. If the odd facades of the units were any representation of the people living in them, then my first year of university was going to be a whole lot more... interesting than I'd expected it to be. I wandered down the hall and turned into the kitchen. A plate of cookies sat on the counter with a note: *Welcome Neighbour.* It was signed, *3B.* Wind chimes.

At least I had one friendly neighbour.

Who apparently had access to my house.

Munching on a snickerdoodle, I worked my way through the rest of the house. One bathroom, two bedrooms, a living room, kitchen and in-house laundry. All the necessities of life, thirty minutes walk from campus.

I'd told my parents I'd be fine in a dorm, but they wouldn't allow it. To hear them tell it, dorms were where you stayed if you didn't want to learn anything at university. The dorm was full of parties and alcohol and girls, and the serious students all stayed off-campus. It didn't sound so bad to me, but they'd paid, so I didn't make a fuss.

I peered out the living room window. What a view. A real collection of nutcases, and my dad thought I'd fit right it.

Family.

You can't live with them...

I turned away from the window to start unpacking my stuff when I saw movement out of the corner of my eye. The curtain in 3A's window was swaying.

I wasn't the only one curious about my new neighbours.

I dumped all my clothes onto the floor of my closet. Now fully unpacked, I decided to take my first solo steps into my new world, and return the cookie plate to Wind Chimes in 3B. Stuffing the last two cookies into my mouth, I stepped out my door and headed right, weaving my way through a melange of woodland creatures. I knocked on the frame of the screen door and waited, my attention drawn to a resin sculpture of what looked like a cross between a turtle and some sort of bear.

"Do you like it? My grand-nephew made it for me."

Startled, I turned back to the door. Standing behind the screen was an elderly woman, the top of her head barely reaching the latch of the door.

"It's... great," I managed. "Very... creative."

"Oh, it's terrible." Her eyes glinted a silver to match her hair. "I think it's supposed to be a pony, but it looks like something the pony might leave behind, if you catch my meaning."

I caught her meaning and laughed appreciatively. She smiled up at me.

"Well, come on in, don't be shy. The rest of that batch is in the jar in the kitchen." She pointed at the plate in my hand and I followed her into the house.

It had exactly the same layout as my unit. But where I had bare walls and open space, my neighbour had filled the rooms with antique furniture that had probably been purchased new. Knick-knacks and figurines sat on crocheted and starched doilies that covered every surface. On the walls were what looked like the entire Bob Ross Signature Collection.

"My name's Grace. Grace Parker. I probably remind you of your grandma. It seems I always remind everyone of their grandma. You know, it used to be that I reminded everyone of their old flame." Her eyes sparkled again. "But that was a long time ago. Now all I can do is wait for the day I remind them of their great-grandma. Until then, grandma will do just fine, thank you very much. Another cookie?"

Realizing that a conversation with Grace did not require active participation, I nodded gratefully and tried the oatmeal raisin.

"And you're Jordan, of course. Oh, don't look surprised. Your father was here to talk to that old blowhard Noah a while ago and was bragging all about his son the genius to whoever would listen to him. And I'm a wonderful listener."

I nodded again, and she passed me the milk.

"So, you're planning on starting classes in a few weeks? Sociology? Interesting field. I was a school teacher myself. 40 years. Saw many a young man such as you start out on the road to knowledge. Do make good use of your time here, won't you? Education is such an important thing. If you ever need anything, you just let me know, alright?"

I swallowed and nodded affirmatively while I brushed crumbs off my shirt.

Grace whisked the plate away. "Well, it's been just grand chatting with you. Feel free to stop by anytime. Oh, and don't play your music too loud, will you dear? Lovely. See you around the courtyard."

I high-stepped it back to my unit, narrowly missing one of Bambi's ears. Grabbing the stack of mail piled on my plastic chair, I swung through the front door and let it close behind me. Grandma Grace in 3B had given me an idea. I tossed the mail onto the coffee table, and turned to dig through my backpack, pulling out a fresh ream of paper. I pinned nine sheets to the living room wall, in a rough horseshoe pattern. There were two weeks until orientation started. Two weeks to do some sociological field work of my own. On the bottom right piece of paper I wrote *1B-Noah*. On second thought I changed it to *Noah/Patton* and then underneath started a list. *Complex manager, grump...* that's all I really had at this point.

One page up was my unit, so I drew a large smiley face. Probably not the most mature piece of art from a man newly out on his own, but I was in an optimistic mood.

Above the smiley face was 3B. *Grace.* Her list was more detailed, as suited our newfound friendship. *Short, cookies, teacher.* I stood back and surveyed my handiwork.

How did I ever get accepted into a university?

Tuesday, August 19

The alarm clock woke me at exactly 8:17 AM, which I thought was odd, as I had set it for 7:30. I stumbled into the living room and flopped into a chair. Yesterday's research smiled at me from the wall.

I gave a grunt reminiscent of Patton, and considered how one's perspective of the validity of one's chosen career path is affected by the hour of the day through which one views it. My morning haze always made me want to drop sociology, and take up product testing. Specifically mattresses.

My gaze wandered from the wall and settled on the pile of unopened mail on the coffee table. How did a new resident get that much mail? I picked up the pile and leaned back, adjusting my plaid boxer shorts for maximum coverage, in case Grandma Grace decided to pop in with another plate of cookies.

Most of it was junk mail. Junk mail. More junk mail. Something for a Henry Davidson. Maybe he'd lived here before me. It was from Russia. I looked at the receiving address. 4A.

Not someone who lived here, then. Someone who lives there, now. I'd gotten his mail by mistake. I set it aside to drop off later.

I continued through the pile. There was more misdelivered mail. A letter from Ottawa for Ian Fox. It was meant for the tenant of unit 1A.

The house of mirrors.

Then it was a bill for Noah in 1B, a selection of catalogues for Grandma Grace in 3B, and some letters for L & S Gordon in 5A, sent from William Head Institution.

Nothing for me. I wondered if someone else in the complex had gotten my mail?

Ok, fine. So I had to go meet some more of my new neighbours. But not until I had a shower. And a coffee. After all, I was an adult now.

I knocked gingerly on the door of unit 1A. There was no answer. I knocked again, a little louder, and turned to look at the lawn. I hadn't dreamt it. It was still a mosaic of mirrors. Walking up to the front door, I'd felt like Indiana Jones, in danger of poison darts if my footing slipped. Even as I stood there and the sun began to beam down above the line of roofs and trees, the mirrors reflected the light into every corner of the courtyard, banishing all trace of shadow and showing off every speck of dirt, fallen leaf, and cobweb. I decided that my front window was in desperate need of a washing. Were those butt-prints?

"Go away!"

The noise startled me. I spun around, expecting to see another little Grace standing at the door, as if this entire complex was populated by stealthy, blue-haired ninjas. But the door wasn't open.

"I said, go away!"

The voice came from deep in the house. It was a man. I peered through the frosted glass in the door's window and saw movement in an opening down the hall. I knocked again and yelled, "I'm sorry to bother you Mr. Fox, but I got some of your mail by mistake—"

"There's no one here!"

This last got me thinking. Should I call him on it? Or just let him be? My morning coffee kicked in.

"That's ok! There's no one out here either!" I mentally patted myself on the back for my cleverness.

"Oh yah, then who's talking?" cried the voice in triumph. I sighed and turned away. Some people just aren't meant to be understood.

"Who are you?" The voice was closer now. "Who sent you?"

I answered, "No one sent me. I got your mail—"

"How did you know my name?" This guy was seriously paranoid.

"Like I said, I got some of your mail by accident," I explained. "I'm just dropping it off for you."

"Did you open it?" He was right behind the door now, and his voice had dropped to a whisper.

"No." I found myself whispering too. "As soon as I saw your name on it—"

"Aha! So you already knew my name!" I could almost smell his irrational brain sizzling.

"No, I mean, when I saw your address, I knew—"

"You know my address too?!" Fox slammed what I can only hope was his hand against the back of his door. "Who are you? Why are you here? Just leave me alone!" His voice receded into the house. I stood at the door, unsure of what to do next. I mean, I'm pretty sure my new neighbour thought I was an alien, or a spy, or something. What do you say to that? *I come in peace.* Or maybe *take me to your leader.*

As enjoyable as playing on his paranoia would have been, I decided to be the "bigger man." I called through the door, "I'll be just across the courtyard if you change your mind."

He wailed in fear. I high-tailed it through the mirrors and across the courtyard. Apparently Ian Fox didn't see me as a "bigger man." He saw me as Big Brother.

If my other stops weren't as strange, they certainly couldn't be called normal. Noah took his mail with a grunt and an all-too-firm handshake. Patton didn't even acknowledge I was there. Grandma Grace accepted her catalogues with a smile, but complained that the winter hedgehog collection was "a trifle cliché, don't you think, dear?"

L & S Gordon turned out to be a pair of middle-aged Amazon women, both of whom came to the door and filled it, squeezing in next to each other but not coming out the other side. I could almost hear the doorframe wincing. They sorted through their prison letters, arranged them in alphabetical order by inmate's last name, and thanked me for my trouble. I told them it was no problem, but they wouldn't let me go without giving me a tip. They called it a gratuity, which I'd never heard of. They found that hilarious. One of them (I think it was S) went into the house to fetch some cash. L stood in the doorway alone and made small talk, carefully weaving the conversation around my clumsy attempts to find out why all of their mail came from a penitentiary.

The doorway caught its breath for a few moments before S came back, crammed herself back into the doorframe, and presented me with a quarter. They retreated back into the house, trading letters and leaving me on the doorstep, paid and forgotten.

They seemed harmless enough, as long as you weren't a doorframe.

My last stop was 4A. Henry Davidson. As I approached the house I heard singing. Loud singing. Loud, *operatic* singing. Now, I'm no expert, and I don't know my Pavarotti from my Groban, but this sounded pretty good to me. I listened carefully, to hear if it was Russian, like the postmark on the letter, but I think it was French. I heard lots of *las* anyway.

Unsure of the proper etiquette for knocking while singing, I waited for a break in the music, tapping my foot in time to the beat, and swaying unconsciously as the singer reached his triumphant conclusion. His final note seemed to float away into the depths of his home, and I found myself hoping he was only pausing for breath. I felt as though I had walked into a book reading only in time to hear the last chapter. But no more music was forthcoming, so I knocked my ovation, and heard footsteps approach.

The door was not opened by an opera singer. I had in my mind created a picture of this particular inhabitant, and he was a large, bearded Italian man in his late 50s, the type of man who could sing high notes in a foreign language while wearing a cape and makeup and still seem more macho than your average action star. I expected to be greeted by breath that smelled like garlic and anchovies and spaghetti and music. But when the door opened, that man was nowhere to be seen. Perhaps he was hiding behind the slight, bespectacled, mousy-looking man who smelled of spearmint gum and Kraft dinner, and looked to be in his early 30s.

"Henry Davidson?" I asked, peering down the hall, looking for capes.

"Yes. How can I help you?" His voice carried no hint of the soaring purity I'd heard earlier, but it seemed as though no one else lived here.

"My name is Jordan Melville? I just moved in?" I realized that I was saying every sentence as a question. I hadn't been to class yet, but I'm pretty sure that the first thing they teach you about sociological field-work is to know your own information before trying to collect anyone else's. Time to focus. Be all that you can be.

[10]

"I think I got some of your mail. From Russia?" Another question. I was going to have to watch myself. "I mean, it's from Russia."

"Finally!" Henry grabbed the letter from my hand, and started to turn back into the house. "Thanks for bringing it by. Welcome to the neighbourhood. See you."

The door closed before I could respond, so I walked back over to my unit. Once I was in the door, I grabbed a pen and started filling out the sheets of paper on the wall with the new information I had collected.

5A-L&S. Roommates? Sisters? Lovers? Jail-mail. Hard on their doorframes. Tips.

4A-Henry. Henry was the most confusing of them all. *French opera + Russian letters + Zen garden = Rick Moranis look-alike?* I wasn't a math major, but that still didn't add up to me. I scowled at the question mark on his page.

1A-Ian. Crazy w/ mirrors. I still had his mail.

I fell into a chair and looked at the letter. Addressee: Ian Fox. Sender: CSIS. CSIS? My paranoid neighbour was getting mail from the Canadian Security Intelligence Service?

Maybe it's true; it's not paranoia if they're really after you.

A million new ideas flooded my mind. Maybe Fox was a spy. Maybe he thought I was sent to watch him, as if attempting to earn a university degree was a just a clever disguise for an extended stake-out. Maybe Grandma Grace really *was* a stealthy, blue-haired ninja, sent to assassinate him, and she was in cahoots with Henry, the international spy who sends codes in French sheet music and is in contact with the Kremlin!

I held the letter up to the light, but it was that special security kind of envelope that doesn't let you look through it. Maybe it was all the spy-thinking, but I was in the kitchen holding a kettle full of water above a slowly heating stove element before I caught myself.

I couldn't steam open someone else's mail! That's a federal offence. It's probably even worse when the mail is from CSIS! What if they found out? What if they came for me? I could simply disappear one day, leaving behind only a bare, swinging light-bulb, a knocked-over chair, and an empty cookie plate, and who would Patton ignore then? No, I had a responsibility to the community. No steam for me.

I ripped the letter open with a butter knife.

Dear Mr. Fox,

It is with great regret and no small amount of surprise that I must inform you that the Canadian Security Intelligence Service is not in the business of assassinating law-abiding Canadian citizens. I too felt the surprise I am sure you are feeling as you read this when I discovered this to be true. As an organization, CSIS officially disapproves of killing of any kind, although when I researched this deeper in order to fully answer your query, I was turned away from the 17th floor, which of course you must know is our "Grey Area," much akin to Harry Potter's Department of Mysteries. I must assume with great suspicion that it was my mentioning of your name that caused me to be rebuffed, while the guards descended on me with metal detectors, tasers, and something that looked suspiciously probe-like. Suffice it to say that I will not put myself into that troubling a situation again, although I am convinced that you are in no immediate danger. However, I would warn you; perhaps it would be best if you slept in a different room tonight. Perhaps your kitchen. I will look in on you from time to time. Please keep your air vents clear of detritus, as it quickly collects and blocks the views of our micro-cameras.

Feel free to write again any time, as it is with the greatest pleasure that we receive your mail. If we had an engineering department with half as much imagination as you, we would be the envy of the entire international intelligence community. As we do not, I am indebted to your inventiveness, and remain,

Yours,

John Haffner
Assistant Director (Intelligence)
CSIS

PS. None of the agents in my department feel that the Girl Guides of Canada are any real threat to you, but we welcome you to maintain a passive surveillance if they attempt to re-enter your complex. You may forward any offending cookies to the address we have provided.

I dropped the letter and burst into laughter. They were humouring him! CSIS was completely aware of my insane neighbour and felt he was harmless enough to let him go on. Not only letting him, but encouraging him! I wiped my eyes. Was this legal? Why was someone as high up the ladder as Haffner playing along with Mr. Crazy-Like-a-Fox? My eyes fixed on the horseshoe of papers pinned to my wall.

Ok. Maybe bored people do weird things.

Wednesday, August 20

I had reset the alarm time last night to 7:30 again. It went off at 6:43. I stared at it malevolently. It stared back. I blinked first and went to the bathroom.

Fifteen minutes later, showered and dressed, I munched on a piece of toast spread liberally with mayonnaise. I needed to stop by the grocery store, pronto.

I stepped into my shoes and out of the door and saw a pile of mail sitting on the sun-warped plastic chair. The top item was a postcard.

It was not addressed to me.

The grocery store would have to wait.

Easing back into my front hallway, I flipped through the mail. Junk. Junk. Some registration paperwork from the University. A bill for Noah from a vet.

It looked like Patton had worms.

There was a thin envelope addressed to a Sasha Sterling in 2A. The house with the perfectly manicured lawn.

Curiosity bubbled up inside me. I wanted to read it. But I hadn't met this person yet. Hadn't even tried to get their mail to them. What were the rules for looking at other people's mail? Did you have to exhaust all other options before you look at it yourself?

Even as I thought it I knew that my curiosity would find whatever justification I needed to take a closer look. So really, by ignoring any qualms I may have had, I was just saving time.

I looked around to make sure no one was watching. My empty unit echoed with the ticking of the refrigerator, assuring me that my moral delinquency would go unseen. I held the envelope to the light. It was a cheque. A big cheque.

$150,000.

Suddenly the envelope felt heavier. 150k. For some reason I felt as though I had just robbed a bank. As though the house was surrounded by police. As though I should lock all the doors and windows and hunker down behind the kitchen table with a shotgun and a list of demands. Fox must be rubbing off on me.

The name on the cheque belonged to an Iranian; Izad Rahimi, whose address was in the downtown core. And in the notation field-

Kidney.

Either my new neighbour sells very expensive pies, or they sell organs on the black market.

I flicked my eyes to the living room wall. *2A-Sasha.* Criminal Mastermind? Maybe I'd leave that one blank awhile.

The last item was the postcard that had been on the top of the pile. It was from Sunny Hawaii (it said so right on the picture) and featured a gorgeous tropical sunset that seemed to be dipping past the horizon, rippling orange waves onto a beach shaded by palm trees. I flipped it over.

Wish I were here.
Jenny.

That was it. No note, no long-winded yet cramped description of everything from the colour of the umbrella in one's drink to the tightness of the shorts worn by the cabana boy. Just, *Wish I were here. Jenny.*

What a strange thing to write. If they weren't there, how did they send the postcard? And if they were there, why wish to be there? Another puzzle for me to add to my list. CSIS, black market organ trafficking, the international opera mystery, incarceration communication, and now coded postcards.

I slumped into my chair. This was getting to be too much. I needed a cookie.

Newly fortified by oatmeal and chocolate chips, I stood next to the fountain, wondering where to go first. Counter-clockwise, I decided.

That's scientific.

Thus satisfied, I headed for 3A, where dwelt the recipient of the mysterious postcard. As I stepped past the draped window to the door, I recalled that this was the unit where I had seen the curtains moving when I first arrived. I didn't know who they were, but they knew who I was.

I knocked loudly, and waited. A shadow appeared at the end of the hall and approached the door. It stopped a few feet away and stood still. No movement or sound emanated from behind the frosted glass while I shifted awkwardly from one foot to the other, not daring to knock again when someone was so obviously right next to the door but choosing not to open it.

I stared at the welcome mat and considered the meaning of irony.

We stood in silence, the shadow and I, until finally a small feminine voice slipped out between the windowpanes.

"You're the new boy." My head snapped up in affirmation.

"Yeah, I just moved in across the way." I gestured behind me, not wanting to look away, positive that the shadow would be gone when I turned back around. "I got some mail that was supposed to come here and—"

"Thank you. You can just leave it on the mat. I'll get it later." The voice was so soft it was almost a whisper.

"Are you sure?" I asked, waving the postcard in the air. "I've got it right here."

Silence from the other side of the door.

I've offended her. I thought. *She's part of some religion that equates waving postcards in the air with murder or grand theft auto or double-dipping your French fry into a communal glob of ketchup.*

I was jolted from my thoughts by the sound of a deadbolt sliding open. The door opened a crack, until it was stopped by the chain. A hand shyly ventured out and I placed the heretical postcard into it. I looked up just in time to catch a fading view of two green eyes gazing through a veil of dark brown hair. Her hand swept her hair back over her ear, and the rest of her shrank back into silhouette.

"Thank you."

The door closed. Her shadow disappeared into the house. I turned back into the bright courtyard and wandered past the bare dirt yard and dead rosebush. I stopped and turned back to the house. The curtains swayed.

She was pretty.

My next stop was the perfectly manicured lawn, sans shrubs, rocks, lawn ornaments, and any clues to the identity of its caretaker. You'd think with this kind of money coming in the mail, they could afford some marigolds, or some birds of paradise, or something. But maybe it was a one-time payoff. They certainly can't donate another kidney. Maybe...

I knocked.

I knocked again. And again.

No answer; no one home. I thought about leaving the cheque under the mat, but the amount made me reconsider. I didn't want to have to answer for a missing cheque for $150,000. It's bad enough having to be responsible for a present cheque for $150,000.

Still no answer. I'd try again tomorrow. After I hit the grocery store.

On to Noah's. He let me in and without asking, poured me a cup of coffee. Black. None of that fancy stuff for him, he said. This was the same coffee he always drank. Drank it in Korea, and drinks it here.

It tasted like it was from the original pot.

Noah shuffled into the kitchen and I took a look around. The interior of his place had been covered in dark wood panelling. The sparse and utilitarian furniture was worn, but well cared for. The walls were bare save for a single framed photograph of Patton. The General, not the dog.

Noah came back from the kitchen with a can in his hand. I handed him the vet bill. He grumbled and told me I should have kept it. He scooped some dog food out of the can and splotched it down into the upside-down army helmet in front of Patton before returning to the kitchen. It was an expensive brand of food.

For the Active Dog.

I looked down at Patton and kept my mouth shut.

"So, how have you been doing with your new neighbours?" Noah's voice bellowed from behind a cupboard door, where he was looking for a small bowl to fill with age-hardened mints.

"Pretty good." I sipped at the scalding coffee, and winced as it removed at least three layers of throat tissue I'd been saving up. "I've met almost everyone, I think, while I've been delivering the mail. Do you know why everyone's mail comes—?"

"Well." With this utterance, Noah sat down at the table and fixed me with a glare.

I paused, unsure of what my response was supposed to be. Noah's eye twitched.

"Well, what?" I tried to grin casually, but my lip trembled. Damn. When I moved out I thought I knew everything; I thought I could conquer the world. Turns out I'm unsure of everything, and can't hold up my end of a normal conversation with a single person in my housing complex.

Such is life.

"You have been doing pretty well with your neighbours, not pretty good. Bad grammar is a pet peeve of mine," said the war veteran. I fought back the urge to salute. "But it's *good* that you're meeting all of them. They're *good* people. I've known most of them for years."

"Yah, I met Grace. She seems really nice, and so does—"

"Nice! Ha! Stubborn, and testy as an old battleaxe. Course, she used to be a real looker, but time steals beauty from the best of us." He smoothed the last remaining stragglers of white hair back over his bald head.

Great. My unit was smack in between a blowhard and a battleaxe. I had just moved myself into the middle of a feud that appeared to having been going on for some time.

I watched Noah mutter about the trouble with women and an idea crossed my mind, took the stairs down, and bolted through my mouth.

"I just met the girl who lives in 3A," I tried very hard not to blush. "Didn't get her name though—"

"Oh that's the Dryden girl. Jenny. Pretty girl. Doesn't get out much. I think she's an arachnophobe."

"She's afraid of spiders?"

"Spiders? How the hell should I know?" Noah glared at me again. I turned to my coffee for help, but it had its own problems. "She's afraid of people. You know, being outside. An arachnophobe."

I wanted to tell him that he meant an agoraphobe, but then I thought it was just as well.

Or just as good.

Either/or.

So I thanked him for the coffee, stepped widely around Patton, and headed home.

There was a note taped to my door.

I see you have been receiving the complex's mail. Has there been anything for me? If so, please drop it off at my door at your earliest possible convenience. (Under the mat is fine.) Thank you.

It was signed: *SS.*

SS. Sasha Sterling. The mystery tenant from 2A. The Master Criminal. I loped across the courtyard and, careful to keep off the grass, knocked on the door. No answer. I waited a while, peering through the windows and knocking sporadically, but still no one came to answer the door.

As uncomfortable as it made me, I bent down and slipped the cheque under the mat, leaving just a corner showing to let them know I'd been there.

I hurried back to my unit, and as I shut the door I saw the front door to 2A close. SS had received the package.

I wasn't sure whether I should be spooked or mix myself a vodka martini; shaken, not stirred. I closed the door and checked and rechecked the locks. Minutes later I was in my bedroom, phoning my father. He had some explaining to do.

My dad was less than helpful. He listened to me ranting about my neighbours, interrupting me periodically to yell out a particularly amusing story to my mother, and failing miserably to contain his laughter.

[19]

That's the thing about my family. You can always count on them for a sympathetic ear. Not that they'd ever act on what they heard. I'm the middle child you see. The *classic* middle child.

My older brother, Troy, is the overachiever. The kind of guy with a trophy shelf in his room that sags from the weight. He was the president of everything, aced everything, and won a scholarship for everything. To my bank manager and legal assistant parents, he was a gift from God. He was almost a god himself.

Now he's a doctor. And not just any doctor.

A brain surgeon.

I'm not kidding. These are the footsteps I'm following in.

My younger sister, Lauren, is the princess. She's the spoiled one that always gets away with everything, usually by blaming it on me. The kind of girl that will flirt her way out of a speeding ticket. After I came along and didn't exceed expectations in any field, she was my parent's last chance and they gave her anything she wanted in the hopes that she would succeed. Piano lessons, dance class, soccer teams during the summer. She can play the oboe and the violin, and just got early acceptance into Julliard's ballet program.

She's in grade 10.

And then there's me. The middle child. The one with a shelf full of participation ribbons. The one who spent a summer mastering the C scale on trombone. The one starting a degree in sociology, because he has no idea what he wants to do with his life. Classic.

Still, my parents never held it against me. I didn't work out, but they had two kids that did, so I was never pressured or made to feel that I was a disappointment. It's easy not to disappoint when nothing is expected of you.

Honestly, I'm thankful. Look at my siblings.

Who wants to compete with that?

So when I called to give my dad an earful about the nuthouse he'd sent me to, he didn't give me a list of reasons why I should try harder to fit in and make friends like my sister would or go the extra mile like my brother would. Instead he just laughed.

"Well, you said you wanted to meet a different kind of people than we have around here."

And I had said that. But I'd meant I wanted to escape suburbia, with its brand new houses and low, passive-aggressive fences, and families with 2.4 kids, a dog, and a minivan.

As I hung up the phone, I looked out the window into the mirrors across the courtyard.

Careful what you wish for.

My stomach growled and the mayonnaise called to me from the fridge. I plugged my ears and went to the grocery store.

Thursday, August 21

The sound of screeching tires woke me up. I rolled over, my face turning to the clock. It said 4:25 AM, and I groaned, pulling my pillow over my head.

Who could be pulling into our courtyard this early in the morning?

Wait.

Pulling *into* our courtyard? Cars don't pull into the courtyard.

They park on the street.

I pulled the pillow off my head. Red and blue lights spun dizzily through the window and chased each other around the walls of my room.

Cops.

I jumped out of bed and headed down the hall. The steady thrum of an idling engine matched the pulse of my veins.

How'd they find out so fast? It was only one letter!

I reached the front door and threw it open, my arms waving frantically in the air in surrender.

But it wasn't the cops.

It was an ambulance.

I stepped outside and saw that many of the other residents were also curious about our emergency visitor. Off to my right, L & S were crushed into their doorframe in matching housecoats, shuffling and manoeuvring for the most advantageous view. Henry was standing out past his Zen garden, fully dressed. He was even wearing a tie. Sasha's house was still dark, but I could just make out a shape standing behind

[22]

the front window. Jenny's house was blocked by the ambulance, the lights of which were in turns illuminating our courtyard red and blue, red and blue.

Fox's house was lit up like an emergency-themed Christmas tree, his mirrors reflecting the flashing lights like a disco ball at a middle school dance. Fox had turned his living room lamp on, and was standing inside with his face mashed up against his front window, looking for all the world like one of those Garfield plush toys with the suction cups on the paws. A mist of breath was slowly spreading out across his window, advancing and receding like a tide of nervous energy.

Noah was leaning out his front door, his face a frozen mask, his skin pulled tight. It looked as though all of his wrinkles had been filled in with fear. I supposed as the complex manager, the health and safety of the tenants were his responsibility.

I turned back to the ambulance, doing the math in my head. L & S, Henry, Sasha, Fox, Noah, me... that left Patton (who I doubt rates a whole ambulance), Jenny, and—

The stretcher was wheeled out of Grandma Grace's house, the attendants careful to lift her over her threshold without bumping her. Her eyes were closed, and her brow furrowed as if in deep thought. As she was pushed across the lawn, one of the paramedics accidently kicked over one of her plaster hedgehogs. It skittered underneath the gurney, its tiny spines snapping off as it bounced under the ambulance and came to a sudden stop against the base of the fountain in the middle of the courtyard.

Broken.

No need to worry until you know what exactly you should be worrying about, isn't that right dear? I could almost hear her voice, chiding me.

I liked Grace. *But what if I want to worry?*

I looked back to the ambulance. As one of the paramedics inserted an IV into Grace's arm, the other jumped out of the back, closed the doors, and turning, scanned the courtyard, surveying the hodgepodge of inhabitants until his eyes came to rest on me.

"Jordan?" His voice made it sound like a question, but his eyes made it a statement. I understood perfectly even as I nodded. He didn't have time to be wrong.

"She said to give you a message. Read them. You can help." He turned away.

Read them? She knew...?

"Is she going to be ok?" He continued on to the driver's side door, climbing in, unable or unwilling to answer the question. He must have heard it a million times.

"Is she going to come back?" I think it was the way I worded it that stopped him. He turned to look at me through the half-closed door. The pain of having answered that question too many times before, having been wrong too many times flashed across his face. Before he could respond, two metallic bangs sounded from inside the ambulance. His partner, signalling him.

Bam! Bam!

No time to waste!

They started to move, and the lights flashing from the roof seemed to heighten their intensity. There was the scratchy rumble of tires pivoting on pavement, the added chaos of a turning signal, and then the circular sound of a fading siren. Fox's mirrors seemed anxious to release the red and blue lights, and within moments all traces of the ambulance were gone.

Gone with Grace.

I stood near my front door, listening to the sound of doors closing all around the complex. Lights flickered off, deadbolts were thrown, and suddenly I was alone. I walked out to the fountain and picked up Grace's hedgehog. It was broken in two, not counting all the little pieces that had come off on its way over.

I followed the trail back to Grace's yard, picking up the pieces as I went. Once I was sure I had them all, I headed back to my door— and saw the pile of mail sitting on the chair.

I stared at it for a full minute. Then, out of the corner of my eye I saw the curtains move in 3A. Jenny was watching.

I took stock for a moment.

Jenny was watching me.

Standing on my front porch, holding a broken lawn ornament and a pile of mail, at 4:30 in the morning.

In my polka-dot boxers.

I walked back inside my unit with the hedgehog and the mail, but left my dignity on the porch for the night. I'd pick it up in the morning, if it was still there.

I sat on the edge of my bed. I didn't know why I felt so... I didn't even know what I felt. Sure, it was sad, but I hardly knew Grace. And one plate of snicker-doodles does not a relationship make. So why did I feel so... involved?

By the time I pulled the blankets over my head I had come up with two reasons.

One, Grace had charged me with a task. I now had a responsibility to her. Simple. And the second reason was simpler. The look on Noah's face.

Maybe Grace was right.

Maybe I could help him.

My alarm went off at 7:30. This would have been a pleasant surprise, had I not set it for 6:30 this time. I rose quickly, got myself brushed and washed, and strode to the kitchen and made a fresh pot of coffee.

I was on a mission today. Help Noah.

But how?

I couldn't very well go up to his door, invite myself in, set him down on his couch and ask him to tell me all about his childhood.

Not my area of expertise, and I'm pretty sure he wouldn't stand for it.

I could ask Patton to tell me what he needed, but I'd bet money that that dog wouldn't give up anything, even under torture.

I don't know if he'd even notice the torture.

Nope, I had to make do with the weapons in my arsenal. This so far consisted of a laptop, a faulty alarm clock, and a pile of mail.

Unopened. For now.

Step One: gather information.

Pouring myself a steaming cup, I headed into the living room. I plunked myself down onto the couch, set the coffee on the floor, and pulled my laptop onto my knees.

I wished I'd been able to bring my smartphone with me, but my parents thought it would be a waste since I didn't have anyone here to call yet. They weren't willing to pay the bill, and I didn't have much money, so a cheap cell-phone and my laptop would have to do, at least for a while.

I was a child of the internet. Having never grown up without it, it was of course the first thing I turned to whenever I had a question about anything. Google, YouTube, Wikipedia. How had people my parent's age survived without them?

Probably by listening to the radio with the whole family late into the night, looking like a picture by Norman Rockwell. Or maybe by running down to the general store for the latest news, drawing moustaches on the wanted posters on the way. Or maybe by huddling around the fire listening to the others grunt and snort while they argued over whether or not the wheel would catch on.

I stored these thoughts away for the next time I called my dad.

My first search led me to a video on how to steam open envelopes without getting them all soggy and wrinkly. Apparently it's all in the wrist. If you hold it at the right angle, at the right distance from the kettle, or pot, or whatever, it'll open like magic, with no one the wiser, as long as you can close it up again. Luckily, ever since kindergarten, my mother had packed my "back-to-school" backpack with everything a crafty little five-year-old could want, including a glue stick. Never mind that I hadn't used one in ages.

I made a mental note not to include her in the general store/wheel joke, as my way of saying thanks.

I slurped back the now-lukewarm coffee and slid the laptop onto the other couch cushion. Step one: complete.

Step Two: practice makes perfect.

I grabbed the stack of mail I'd brought in early this morning and flipped through it. Junk mail and mail for me in the Practice Pile. Mail for anyone else in the Perfect Pile. Fate smiled on me; there was a form letter from the municipality informing everyone about a community meeting regarding the rezoning of an empty lot seven blocks away. It struck me as unlikely that any of my neighbours would be attending. That was nine pieces for the Practice Pile.

Nothing for me, but Noah, Sasha, and Jenny each had a letter, and there was a small stack of mail for L & S, tied together with string. Together, they comprised the Perfect Pile.

Thus sorted, I brought the two piles into the kitchen and set them on the counter, then set a pot of water to boil. I rushed out of the room to put on some clothes. I had recently become aware that my habits of undress gave my neighbours reason to think that *I* was the strangest tenant in the complex.

I stood in front of my closet, contemplating what kind of image I wanted to project to the others. All-business, like Henry? Competent and unapproachable, like Noah? Mysterious like Sasha, insane like Fox, invisible like Jenny? I decided to avoid Grace's matronly look and L & S's perfect coordination and dug through the pile of clothes on the floor, threw on a semi-clean T-shirt and shorts, and got back to the kitchen just as the water started boiling.

My first attempt was a dismal failure. I threw what was left of Grandma Grace's form letter into the garbage, where it landed with a wet thump, blurring its letters and numbers into an unreadable clump of bureaucratic paper maché.

The next three were the same, with little-to-no improvement. Mail destined for Fox, Jenny, and myself all followed the path Grace's had forged, dripping themselves into the trash. I adjusted my angle and height.

Sasha's was better, it opened and was readable, but still in no condition to be resealed. Noah's and Henry's were the closest of all. They opened cleanly, and the steam had no effect on the letter inside, but the flap was wrinkled; a dead giveaway. Still, they gave me hope. L & S's was looking to be perfect; a clean open with no wrinkles and no water-spots, easily sealable.

The perfect crime.

Until I dropped it into the pot.

I gingerly hoisted it over to the garbage can, hearing a taunt in each drip.

No more mister nice guy.

The vacant unit, 4B, was my last chance. It was addressed, "Occupant," so technically I was still breaking the law by opening it, but

I figured at this point it was probably the least illegal thing I'd done today, so I didn't hesitate.

And it was perfect.

Troy, eat your heart out.

I took out the letter, leaving the envelope to dry on the dish rack. Checking it for water spots, I found it had none, so I set it aside and headed to my room for the glue stick.

I set the stick on the counter, picked up the envelope, and walked through the house waving it gently back and forth as if I were skimming my fingers over the surface of a pond. When I deemed it dry enough, I went back to the kitchen and set it on the counter. The form letter folded back into its original shape and slid easily into the envelope. I applied a careful strip of glue to the fold and, using a ruler from my "back-to-school" kit, gently smoothed the flap down into its original place.

Perfect. The nonexistent occupant would never know.

Now to business.

Step Three: interference with Her Majesty's Mail. I almost stopped to think about the illegality of what I was doing, of what I was about to do, but the look on Grace's face as they wheeled her to the ambulance was overpowering.

Read them.

My mind made up, I turned to the second pile.

The Perfect Pile.

I honestly wasn't sure if Grandma Grace had meant read everyone's mail, or just hers, but I figured better safe than sorry.

I looked at all the different options, and my curiosity got the best of me. Sasha's first.

It was thin. Similar to the first one, the one with the cheque, but this one had a letter in it. I steamed it open and set the envelope on the dish rack to dry. Unfolding the contents carefully, I held it away from the steam, and wandered into the hallway. It was a letter of enquiry, responding to a classified ad.

Dear S. Sterling,

I'm writing in response to your advertisement in the Times Colonist, dated August 16th. I am very interested in your Soviet world map. I would like to inspect it before I purchase it, of course. Please let me know of a time that would work for you, and I'll come see it.

I do have a few questions about it. Is it the 1962 edition that doesn't include Iceland? Also, what colours are used for China and Panama?

I have never replied to an ad by mail before. It seems unusual. Please feel free to call me at (250) 555-2497, as I am anxious to purchase this item.

Dr. Barnaby Hender

I'd ended up back where I started; in the kitchen. I set the letter down. At least it wasn't a kidney.

I turned to Jenny's letter. It had been sent from Hawaii, just like the postcard. A bubble and hiss later, and I had it in my hands, the envelope set to dry next to Sasha's.

Dear Jenny,

I hope this letter finds you well. I'm feeling much better since the last time I wrote. I guess that's what vacations are for, right? Well, Hawaii is nothing like Seattle. When it rains, it rains warm. Yesterday it just started pouring in the middle of the day, and I went out and walked in it all along the beach. The tourists (I don't consider myself a tourist, even though I clearly am one. I think it's because I refuse to wear straw hats and fanny packs) all rushed back to their hotels to wait it out, but I just walked in it. It was so warm, like walking through a shower. Which I guess is just what it is! Isn't it funny that we never think of them that way up in the Northwest? Maybe it's because they're cold showers there. Well, here they don't have cold showers. Nothing that will wash away their passion for life. That's what it is here, that's why I feel better. They have a passion for life. Not just for excitement, not the way we think about it. For life. For food, and good company, and going out and staying in, and singing, and praying, laughing and crying. Life. I know you'd like it here. Not in the city maybe, not with the tourists. But on the empty beach, standing in the rain with me. Maybe someday, right?

But I'm not preaching to you. I know you hate that. For now, just read my letters. I told my doctor about them, and he thinks they're just as good for me as they are for you, so... I guess everybody wins.

I love you, sis.

Cathy

PS. did you get the postcard? I can't believe I brought it all the way down here with me! Next time I'm buying you one locally, and you can wait to write on it when it gets to you! Hugs!

I wasn't sure which was worse; the fact that I had so intruded into this girl's life, or the fact that I was thrilled to have new information about her. I mean, this whole thing was supposed to be about me helping Noah. How does this help Noah? I set her letter aside. I was losing sight of my good intentions. Noah was next. Time to get back on track.

To: Lt Colonel (ret) Noah M. Foster,
Dear Sir,

Please allow me to express my regret over your decision not to appear at the unveiling of the Korean War Veterans Memorial this Remembrance Day. Your presence and approbation will be sorely missed.

Though you made it clear that you did not want to participate in the ceremony, I would like to invite you to attend as a civilian, nonetheless. You would do great honour to us and to the memory of those we seek to recognize. Please consider it.

Lest we forget,

Jack Cardinal
President, Pacific Region, Korea Veterans Association of Canada

I folded the letter, and quietly sat down onto the couch. For some reason I felt that it would be disrespectful to do anything else. Even though I had known that Noah was a war veteran, it had never really sunk in. I suppose I imagined him standing in an old army camp, surrounded by drab olive-coloured tents, wringing his laundry out over a large metal drum while smoking a cigar and grunting in disappointment at the new recruits.

Watch where you're swinging that kit of yours, son.

It never occurred to me that Noah could have been one of those soldiers we saw on video in Social Studies, surrounded by mud, blood, and camouflage nets. To be honest, I didn't even remember studying the Korean War. World War II, sure, and Vietnam, absolutely. But not the war in between. The invisible war.

But not invisible to Noah, I bet.

He probably couldn't stop seeing it.

Grace's command swept back into my mind.

Help.

Right. How could I help him? Obviously he didn't want to go, and I didn't really feel up to hosting a *White Christmas*-style reunion in our complex. Although it would give Noah a chance to fire up the BBQ for the first time.

It struck me that the best way for me to help Noah might be for me to leave him alone.

I wondered what Grace would think of that.

I resealed the letters.

I wasn't up to opening all of the letters in L & S's package, and I didn't have any string to retie them with, so I left them in one piece, but did check out the return address.

Vancouver Island Regional Correctional Centre.

And the name of a different inmate on every one.

Next time, I swore to the letters. *Next time, you're mine.*

The opened letters had resealed beautifully, so I picked them up with the pack for L & S, and slipped into my shoes.

Step Four: Delivery.

First up was Noah. I didn't feel up to chatting with him today, not after reading his letter. I'm sure he would have known something was wrong, and if he hadn't noticed, Patton would have clued him in.

I left the letter on the chair by Noah's door.

Next, Sasha. It occurred to me, as I was slipping the letter under the mat, that I had no idea whether Sasha was male or female. The items she/he sold didn't give any clues. After all, everyone should have a kidney, and no one should have a Soviet map of the world.

Then Jenny. Again, I didn't have the heart to face her, and after reading her letter, I'm reasonably sure she didn't have the heart to face me. Or anyone else for that matter. She sent *herself* postcards, for pete's sake. How isolated can you get?

Finally, I stopped off at L & S's place. Here I knocked, and heard the two residents yelling back and forth in response;

"Oh! Someone's at the door!"

"I heard them Louise!"

"Well, are you going to answer it?"

"You're closer, you answer it!"

"I'm busy!"

A pause.

"Fine, we'll both answer it."

Twin shuffles made their way to the front door, and it was opened by two hands, one from Louise, and one from the unknown "S." One pulling on the door handle, and the other steadying the frame for what was to come.

It came.

Both of them squeezed into the doorframe, each letting out a *huffff* that sounded like a kneeling camel and smelled like an Italian sausage. They looked at me quizzically for a moment, and then the face on the right one brightened in recognition.

"Oh Sylvia, it's the boy from down the way. The one in his underwear!"

Sylvia stared at me critically, as if she were wondering what possible motive I could have had for wearing something more than boxer shorts today, and thereby confusing her. I interrupted her silent shaming.

"I brought you your mail."

"Oh of course, our mail. Just like last time." Sylvia frowned suddenly. "I suppose you'll be wanting another tip?"

I assured her that this was a service I was willing to provide for gratis, a word that pleased her immensely, and they ushered me into the house.

The two women bounced off each other down the hallway, neither one taking the lead, both of them making overlapping excuses as to why the house was in no condition for visitors, and please excuse them for the mess, and would I like some tea?

I interjected an affirmative between an undying refrain of "—promised she would finish that puzzle in '89, but here it sits!" and "If only Louise would use some of those coupons, we wouldn't have to keep all those shoeboxes!" and the tea arrived, with biscuits.

Louise and Sylvia, it turned out, were sisters. They'd moved into the house in 1984, and as far as I could tell, hadn't unpacked a box since. There were boxes stacked all along the walls and in between the pastel-coloured furniture in the place of end tables. I was politely trying to keep from dripping a soggy biscuit on a box marked "Alcatraz: 1979-1983," and Sylvia caught me staring at it.

"Oh, those are old letters from inmates." She took a sip of her tea. I waited, but there was no more explanation to come. I went on the offensive.

"Did you know them from somewhere?" *Like the crazy murder cult you were a part of, or the heist team you joined, or the Amazon Woman Mafia you ran?* Suddenly I didn't feel like drinking any more tea.

"Not really." Louise dipped a biscuit. "Not as well as we'd have liked to, anyways." She giggled like a little schoolgirl, and Sylvia joined in. I put my biscuit down and brushed the crumbs off my lap.

"Well, I've really got to be going—"

"Oh please, sit down." Louise was all business again.

Sylvia practically chugged her tea. I could almost see the steam coming out of her ears. She spoke.

"Here's the deal. We'd like to offer you a job."

I was taken aback. "A job?"

Louise gazed serenely at the biscuit in her fingers. "We've been watching you Jordan. You're young, energetic, and innocent looking. Just the kind of help we can use."

Sylvia let out the camel sound again and savagely dipped her biscuit into her tea. "Although I'd be more comfortable if you had a bit of muscle on you." Louise turned and shushed her. I had the feeling this was their first disagreement since 1984, and Sylvia knew exactly where to place the blame.

Louise shifted her focus to my face. "Now, what I'm going to tell you is highly confidential. Can we trust you to be..." Louise lowered her voice to a whisper, "*discreet?*"

I nodded, unsure of whether or not I wanted to hear what I was about to hear.

Louise didn't drag out her explanation. "We want the money."

I choked on my tea. "The money? What money?"

Sylvia rolled her eyes. "If you're going to tell it, tell it right, Louise." She turned to me and stage-whispered in confidence, "she's not much of a story-teller."

Louise made the camel noise and rattled her teacup.

"Oh, about 30 years ago, we decided that we didn't want to work in a cubicle anymore, so we quit, and decided to find—"

"Other methods of remuneration." Louise rejoined the storytelling process. They proceeded to finish each other's sentences while I pondered the image of the two of them crammed into a single cubicle, one of them answering phones and crunching numbers while the other clipped coupons and organized them alphabetically into gigantic piles of shoeboxes.

"We came to the conclusion that convicts—"

"Especially bank robbers—"

"Often hid their loot before they went 'inside'—"

"They always do on TV—"

"So we started a letter-writing campaign, and we wrote to all the thieves we could find—"

"And told them that if they told us where to dig—"

"Proverbially—"

"Yes, where to dig, proverbially, we would invest their money for them—"

"Taking only a small handling fee for ourselves—"

"As would be our right."

They both huffed and sat back in their chairs. Sylvia gazed at me appraisingly. Louise got up to refill the teacups.

"But no one... I mean, has anyone...?" I wasn't sure what to say. How does a guy ask if his hostesses are Accessories After the Fact?

I needn't have worried.

"Oh yes, we've made a good living out of it, haven't we, Louise?"

"Oh yes. Very good." Louise returned with a fresh pot of tea, and refilled all the cups. I looked down at the plate in front of me. The biscuits were gone.

"So... what now?" I was at a loss. Were they going to kill me, now that I knew their secret?

"So, now you know." Sylvia added some sugar to her tea and stirred it slowly, eyeing me over the lip of her cup. "The question is... what are you going to do about it?"

"Do?"

"Yes. Do. We just told you something that you can never un-know. So now you have a choice."

Louise chimed in. "You can either turn us in—"

"There might even be a reward—"

"Oh, do you think so?"

"Sh. Or—"

"You can not."

They both nodded, a sharp nod. A physical punctuation.

I felt their eyes on me, and my mind flew back to the ninth grade. I had been standing at the intersection of two hallways in my school, wasting time during the lunch break. I had already eaten my PB&J, and had nothing else to do, what with it being a Wednesday and all. Most of my friends were in some sort of club or group, and all the clubs and groups met on Wednesday at lunch. Student council, chess club, drama club, pep squad, you name it. But I had never been a regular kid. I didn't have any special talents. My Wednesdays were always free.

So there I was, standing alone, when at the end of the hallway a door opened. The door to the boy's washroom. Three boys and a cloud of smoke burst out. The boys, coughing and laughing, hurried down the hallway out of sight. The cloud lingered, as if it were the rejected friend, used up and then left behind until it was next needed.

I was comparing our fates, the cloud's and mine, in the pseudo-poetical way of middle-school martyrs when I heard a whisper of movement behind me and when I whipped around I was standing face to chest with vice-principal Trent. He always turned up at the wrong time.

"Come with me, Melville."

Sitting in his office, I was fixed with a glare. He placed his hands on the desk, and then shifted them to his chin, and then onto the arms of his chair. Restless hands. Craving a chance to punish something.

He spoke: "Did you see who it was?" No other words. No other words were needed. He knew I knew. And he knew that he only had to give me the one opportunity to rat. His hands slowly rose until they hovered over the space between us.

Full of blame that needed a place to settle.

My choice.

I felt that now. Uncomfortably mashed between Alcatraz and Sing-Sing, looking into the twin eyes of the two most inexplicable women I'd ever met, I could feel that choice hovering in the space between us.

I chose.

"You've forgotten one option."

They each raised one eyebrow in anticipation. Louise the left, Sylvia the right. Together they were the very picture of surprise.

I cleared my throat. "I *could* blackmail you both, and take all the money in exchange for not turning you in."

There. It was out.

Where was Mr. Trent when you needed him?

Sylvia looked at Louise. Louise looked at Sylvia. They nodded. Turning in unison, they stared at me. Hard.

Sylvia cleared her throat. "We are prepared," she murmured, "to give you a *reasonable* cut—"

"Providing—"

"Providing, of course, that you do not open *our* mail."

I was shocked. And I must have looked it, because Louise smiled at me beatifically and said, "Oh of course we know, Jordan. All that steam on your kitchen window this morning? What else could it be? You don't cook." She leaned in conspiratorially. "You should remember, we try to think like criminals."

[36]

"But... why? If this has been working for so long, what do you need me for?"

Louise and Sylvia both settled their eyes on me. "That," said Sylvia mysteriously, "is exactly the point."

I was outside the door, staring down the courtyard before I knew it. What kind of an answer was that? I stood on the doorstep, puzzled, when I realized. From this house, you can't see my kitchen window. Then how did they...?

Maybe I should cover them with something. Just in case.

I slowly walked back to my unit. Fox's mirrors caught my eye again, and I noticed for the first time the aluminum foil that papered the windows down the side of his house.

I laughed. I *was* one of them.

The rest of the day I filled with chores and errands. Items of little importance, lost in the haze of unpacking, drowned out by my recent rash of criminal activities.

I wanted to tell my father I was finally the first in our family to do something. Committing a federal offence is something, after all. But if I did, he'd probably just confess that my brother has been secretly painting forgeries of the great masterworks of our time.

And Troy's version of the Mona Lisa really outshines that other guy's work.

I went out and bought blinds. The horizontal ones that cover the windows completely, but still let you peek out to surreptitiously view your surroundings. I also bought a pair of binoculars, some krazy glue, and a kettle that didn't whistle when it boiled, so my other neighbours wouldn't become suspicious.

My final purchase was a horrendously ugly picture of what was either three ducks swimming on a pond or a gang of dwarves performing Riverdance. But it was large enough to cover the space on the wall that held my papers.

I was in business.

Next I unpacked the rest of my boxes. I had to look settled. It would be less suspicious that way. My life of crime demanded it.

As I was sitting at my kitchen table, humming the Get Smart theme song and carefully gluing the spines back onto Grace's hedgehog, I wondered for a moment how it had come to this. Is this the normal life path for someone my age? Middle school, summer camp, high school, summer jobs, stealing mail, black market retail, withholding evidence for personal gain, and then it's off to university!

Somehow I doubted it. I wondered if the novelty of doing something un-average was contributing to my delinquency.

I dabbed a bit more glue on the hedgehog's nose and shifted it to the left so it wouldn't block his cheery smile.

Could be worse.

I finished gluing the hedgehog back together. It wasn't the prettiest hedgehog, but at least it would be ready for when Grace came back home. I didn't allow myself to think of the *if*. She did remind me of my grandma.

Keep busy. Read them. Help Noah.

Time to update the files.

I lifted the picture off the wall and looked at the scribbles I'd written on the pages.

Cookies. Grump. Tips. French Opera. Mirrors. A lot had happened since then. I crumpled up the papers and started fresh. As I filled in the information I had, and added all of the unanswered questions, I realized that the more I knew about these people, the less I understood.

I looked at the blank page that had my name on it.

Oh well. At least I was in good company.

Friday, August 22

I'd set my watch alarm for 7:00 AM. It went off in my right ear exactly when my alarm clock went off in my left. I made a mental note to write a nasty letter to the inventor of the alarm clock. But not too nasty.

Chances are someone else would read it first.

In what was becoming a daily routine, I got out of bed, brushed my teeth, had a shower, and brewed a cup of coffee while I looked over the day's mail. I opened a tuition receipt from the university and a card from my mother.

It was a housewarming card, with some heartfelt gibberish stamped in cursive on the inside, but I could hardly see past the picture on the front.

It was the same picture I had up on my wall. The title was written on the back of the card. *Transient Sunlight*, by Fray Paschal. I glanced back at the picture. My sister used to tell me I didn't appreciate art because I didn't have an artist's soul.

If having an artist's soul would make me appreciate *Transient Sunlight*, I didn't want one.

There were eleven other pieces today. A letter for Henry, this time from Argentina. He does get around. A letter for Fox, from CSIS again. And nine flyers from Walmart.

I started with the flyers. The night before, as I was brushing my teeth, I'd thought to myself, *how am I going to help Noah? By reading his mail?* If that's what Grace had meant, then by opening up everyone else's mail, was I obligated to help them too? I'm pretty sure she'd say yes. She seems like the type who would help people whether she was reading their mail or not.

Goody two-shoes.

So, I thought of a brilliant plan.

I would clip coupons. Just like Louise and Sylvia. No one read these flyers, they just chucked them, so if I took them, and passed around coupons that people might want... no harm, no foul.

Helpful.

Sure, I wasn't bringing about emotional catharsis, or reuniting anyone with their lost loved ones, but it was a start. For an 18 year old, cutting coupons is pretty saintly.

$3.00 off a puzzle mat. That one would find its way into Louise and Sylvia's next batch of con-mail. 50¢ off a standard roll of aluminum foil. I'd stick it in the crack in Fox's door. 20% off dog food (*For the Active Dog*). It would magically appear in Patton's food dish. I set the water to boil and sat happily clipping away when I heard a knock at my door.

I opened the door to find Sylvia, sans Louise. She looked so lonely there, crammed into the left half of my doorway that I almost invited her in. She didn't give me time to speak, which was lucky, because the picture was down off the wall, and my sheets of paper were in plain view had she taken one step further.

"Here." She thrust an envelope into my hand. Without Louise to spur her on, Sylvia's natural sharpness became more noticeable. I wondered how I could ever have thought them indistinguishable?

"What's this?"

"It's your first pay-cheque." She didn't let go as I pulled the envelope towards myself. "It was a slow month. Don't get greedy."

I raised my eyebrows in defence. She sighed and released the envelope.

"You're welcome."

With that, she turned away and marched back to her house, veering slightly to the left and self-correcting the whole way there.

I closed the door and tore into the envelope. The cheque fell out into my hand.

$300.00

And all I'd had to do was eat biscuits. Easiest money I ever made. I set it on the coffee table and marvelled at the criminal life.

The water was ready, so I grabbed the unopened mail and headed into the kitchen. Work beckoned.

Henry's letter was simple. It consisted of a single piece of paper, on which were written the words, *Opening. Knight to e3* in a strong hand. I double-checked the address.

Argentina.

First Russia, and now Argentina.

Henry was an international chess player. Chess by mail.

The name on the return address was Régulo Ibarra. I quickly looked him up online. And there he was. Régulo Ibarra. Argentinean Chess Grand Master. You don't play a Grand Master unless you're good. Really good. I wrote a note and stuck it onto the fridge.

Buy chess set. This game I wanted to see. I just had to figure out a way to see Henry's moves too.

Fox's letter was from the same fellow at CSIS. Apparently they had quite a conversation going.

Dear Mr. Fox,

> *I feel as though it is important for me to remind you that while I cannot necessarily ensure your safety, I can certainly guarantee that your violent death will not come at the hands of the Sisters of Saint Mary of the Cross. We have been watching them for some time now and believe that they would not dare to face off with such a high-level threat to themselves as you are. They contract that sort of thing out to the Sisters of the Good Samaritan.*

> *While this may not ease your mind, I can offer you some consolation. I have been in contact with other senior members of this Service (I cannot tell you their names, of course) who all agree that your work on the secret alliances of World War I was a remarkably unpredictable look at the German/British war machine and certainly explains why Togo was so unexpectedly not the victor of that particular conflict. We recommend that you submit it for publication immediately, although if I were you I would try to sneak it is as fiction, so they don't see it coming.*

As always, it is a pleasure to continue our correspondence. I look forward to tomorrow's letter with great anticipation, and am ever,

Yours,

John Haffner
Assistant Director (Intelligence)
CSIS

I left the envelopes to dry and went out to buy a chess set.

I stepped out of the bank with my chess set under my arm, blinking away the remnants of artificial light. I had just finished setting up my first private account. An account that couldn't be accessed by my parents.

Forget drinking coffee. This was what made me an adult. A solid $300 of my own money, made in my own way. For some reason it felt like it was *my* money, for the first time. Like all the other money I'd ever had had been someone else's.

Let's face it. My allowance was never really *my* money. Even when they gave it to me the week I forgot to take out the garbage, or clean my room, or mow the lawn, it was still my parent's money. They just gave it to me like I was a good little boy, knowing that I would go spend it on junk food, or comic books, or Pokémon cards. In hindsight, it was so patronizing it's insulting.

And my first job was the same. Sure, I was working for it, and it was real money, which I could tell because the government found it worth its while to take some of it, but after all, my dad got me that job. And while caddies made good tips, every time someone tipped me and said, "Tell your dad I said hi," I felt like the money didn't really belong to me.

It was the same story at every place I've worked. Somehow, it never was mine. All I could think of when I looked at my bank account was that I was living at home rent-free and eating home-cooked meals and driving my father's car. I always had cash, but I felt obligated.

Even now, my parents are paying for my place at Stony Creek Estates, but thankfully there is no way that this $300 is connected to them. They're paying for my rent, but I'm paying for school, and they told me before I left that the only repayment they were interested in was me getting a good education.

So, I'm off the hook.

Besides, if they knew where the money was coming from, they'd want no part of it.

Personal justification complete, I breathed in deeply like a man just released from prison. Clean air and an unused chequebook.

True freedom.

I was turning away from the bank doors when I heard my name being called out from across the street. I peered through the blurry fence of traffic and saw Henry waving at me from outside a post office. He was next to a stack of four boxes that seemed dangerously close to falling onto a parked Toyota, and he was flitting around them nervously, shifting them first one way and then another, trying to keep them from toppling. He looked like a wiry, frantic hummingbird.

I weaved my way across the crosswalk to his side.

"Hi... Jordan, right?" I nodded in the affirmative and steadied the boxes. They were sitting half on and half off the curb.

"Right. Would you mind giving me a hand? I have to get these back to our place, and I don't have a car." He paused, looking up at me to measure my level of compassion. I must have looked sympathetic, because he immediately said, "Thanks!" and taking the top box, started down the sidewalk towards home.

I hoisted the other three and followed, trying to catch up and watch my foot placement at the same time. "So... what are we carrying?" I hoped that I wasn't prying, but seeing as I was carrying more than half, I figured I had the right to know.

Henry blushed and mumbled an answer.

"Sorry?" I stumbled over a crack in the pavement as we rounded a corner and was immediately entangled in the leash connecting an overweight old Dachshund to an underweight old man. By the time I had disengaged, Henry was half a block ahead, having not noticed my falling behind. He was talking up a storm, explaining himself to the air, and when I finally caught up to him I was only able to catch the last few gasps of what appeared to be a marathon run-on sentence.

"...and so I did it, rented a space and laid some tracks down, just playing around, you know, and I ordered what the guy told me was an average order but was actually too many as it turns out and now I've got all these boxes of them and this is only the first shipment of four and I'd appreciate it if you didn't tell anyone about this because in hindsight it's all very embarrassing." He turned to me, both of us wheezing from lack of air.

So. He built model trains. Compared to the rest of us, that was almost boring. I tried to give him a look that conveyed understanding and he sighed in appreciation.

"Thanks, Jordan."

We turned into the gate of Stony Creek, both of us averting our eyes to the right to avoid Fox's mirror-shock. I followed Henry past the fountain and around the Zen garden to his front door. To my surprise, he stepped in, carefully holding it open for me to enter behind him. I wiped my shoes on the mat and headed inside.

Henry had me bring the boxes into one of his offices. I say one of his offices because both bedrooms were offices. Each had at least one desk, two computers, and an assortment of monitors. Bundled wire snaked across the floors from one room to the next, creating tripping hazards everywhere I walked, but Henry stepped lightly over them with his box and placed it gently next to an overflowing desk. As I set the other three down, he headed back out into the hallway.

"Sorry about the wires. I work from home, so everything's a bit of a mess." His voice turned the corner into the living room.

"No problem," I called back, taking my chess set from the pile and following him. "Do you want me to open—"

I turned the corner and stopped short, my mouth hanging open. The living room had no computers, no desks, and no wires crisscrossing the floor. It was completely empty, save for a brass music stand in the centre of the room, and an enormous stereo system taking up the far wall.

The *entire* far wall.

Henry came at me with a $20 bill in hand. Seeing the look on my face, he glanced back at the wall behind him. "Oh." He blushed again. "This is where I practice."

Choruses of French opera rushed through my head. I'd heard this stereo play before. And Henry's voice not only matched it in volume and clarity, he *exceeded* it.

Suddenly the boxes made sense. Not model trains at all.

CDs.

Henry had rented a recording studio, laid down the tracks on an album, and now had four boxes of CDs in his house. The first of four shipments. That's 16 boxes. I did the math; about 120 CDs per box based on the size and weight, times 16 boxes... that's almost 2000 CDs.

I tried to imagine Henry's voice times 2000. He almost had enough disk drives to play them all.

He put the cash into my hand. I protested, but he wanted to thank me for helping him with the boxes. In fact, since I had nothing to do until school started, maybe I would like to pick up the next shipment with him when it arrived? The same payment of course.

"It should be one week from today?" he said hopefully. "Wouldn't interfere with school at all?" Now Henry was starting to talk all in questions. I tore my eyes from the wall and focused.

"Sure. But instead of the money, can I have a CD?" His eyes widened.

"Ummm, well... I hadn't really planned on... I mean, if you really want one... but you can't get too critical, it's my first..." His voice trailed off. "You really want one?"

He desperately needed to be appreciated. The signs were all there. He was operating under the assumption that no one thought he was any good. In my experience there was only one way that can happen.

No one had ever told him he was.

"Sure! I heard you singing a few days ago, just in passing, and I thought you were terrific! Really, really good!" Henry's face brightened at the praise, and he rushed to get a copy from the other room. I turned to leave the room and noticed one more item in the room. In the corner to my left was a long, low table supporting five chess sets.

The sets ranged in style; one was glass, and one marble. There was a bronze set, with one half of the pieces burnished to a brighter gleam, and a wooden set that was obviously antique. The fifth was a plastic set, similar to the one in the box under my arm. Three of them were obviously mid-game. The bronze and plastic sets were untouched, but a sense of purpose was settled on them, like I imagined one would feel in an ancient army camp when preparing to go into battle. I knew what the first move of that war would be.

Opening. Knight to e3.

I heard the cool slice of a knife breaking the tape on the CD box.

"I'm going to sign it for you!" Henry's nerves and unease had given way to excitement at the possibility that someone could value his talent. I understood completely. Sharing what we have with someone who will really get it. It was just like me and my coupons. I glanced again at the stereo.

Ok, maybe not *just* like.

Henry wandered into the kitchen, looking for a pen. He shuffled aside two laptops and found a thick black Sharpie. As he was scribbling his John Hancock, I stepped into the hallway again, bumping against a thick bundle of cords.

"Henry, if you don't mind me asking, why do you have so many computers?" I followed the wires with my eyes as they branched off into various rooms down the hall. Henry's voice was at my elbow.

"My work is... complicated." He took a deep breath. "See, I run the technical departments of a few companies, so I need to have constant access to all their networks, and all the networks have to be independent of one another and some companies have more than one network, or have networks in more than one language and I like to have them separated too, 'cause switching back and forth confuses me and also I like computers."

"Henry..." I wasn't sure how far I could push the boundaries of our newfound friendship. "How many companies do you work for?"

He blushed again. "Nine."

"Shut. Up." Henry gaped at me, and I apologized. "Sorry, but... nine? And you run them?"

"Just the technical departments." He started to hold his head a little higher. He was obviously proud of his work.

"And what exactly do the technical departments do?"

"Well..." He faltered again. "It's technical."

I was staggered at the logistics. Nine companies, all at the same time?

An image of Henry, dressed in slacks, a shirt, and a tie at 4:30 in the morning burst into my head.

"Henry..."

"Yes?" He was back in the kitchen, pouring a glass of water.

"Are all of the companies in the same time zone?"

Henry drained the glass. "No." He smiled. "They aren't even all in the same country."

I was shepherded to the door, my time was up. But I had one last question.

"Then... how many languages do you speak?"

He grinned wickedly, enjoying the attention for what was clearly the first time in a long time. "Seven. And I can sing in three more."

He noticed the box under my arm as he gently ushered me out. "Oh, chess! We should play sometime!" The door closed.

Not likely.

Henry Davidson was a genius. A master linguist. A chess Grand Master. And I had his CD.

I looked down at the case in my hand. Decorating the cover of Henry Davidson's self-titled album was Fray Paschal's *Transient Sunlight*.

I decided maybe I wouldn't mind having the soul of an artist after all.

I got home and went straight to the kitchen. Both Henry's letter and Fox's were dried and ready for resealing. As I smoothed the line of glue onto the envelopes, I decided I wasn't going to go back over to Henry's. I'd fed his damaged ego enough for one day. And as for Fox...

Fox was outside.

I could see him through the living room window. He was on his lawn, kneeling on all fours, holding something in his hand that looked like a power tool. I'd spent some time thinking about how to approach him and I didn't want to miss this opportunity, so I grabbed his letter, hurried to the door, and then walked over to his unit as nonchalantly as possible. I landed somewhere between an amble and a mosey.

Fox had his back turned to me, and he was muttering under his breath. As I got closer, I heard the tune he was singing:

Twinkle, twinkle, little star,
You can't watch me from afar.
All the day and all the night,
All you see is shining light.
Twinkle, twinkle, in the skies,
Choke on this, YOU DIRTY SPIES!!!

This last was shouted at the heavens and accompanied by a shaken fist. As he raised his voice and face to the skies, I got my first good look at Ian Fox.

He seemed to be in his fifties, with salt & pepper hair styled in a look reminiscent of Einstein. An unkempt beard hung in scraggles down his face, long in some places, and shaven almost to the skin in others. He was wearing red and gold striped pyjama bottoms, a bright yellow raincoat, and no less than three wedding rings.

He was just as I'd imagined him to be.

When he finished his cry to the universe, I applauded wholeheartedly. He spun around, jumping to his feet as he did so, and threw up his hands.

I peered innocently over the dust-buster which was still gently whirring in his hands.

"Ian?" He blinked. "Ian, it's me, Jordan." I said it slowly and carefully. "Do you remember?"

He blinked again.

"I live just over there. You asked me to collect your mail for you, so they wouldn't know you were home. Remember?"

Fox raised one eyebrow and lowered the dust-buster. "You've been collecting my mail?"

"Yes. See, I have this piece here with me. It has your name on it." I slowed my words down. "Your name is Ian F—"

"Oh shut up, kid. I know my name." Fox snatched the letter from me and examined it. His eyes weaved wildly around the envelope, and I started to sweat. If anyone was going to notice my tampering, it would be Fox.

"Seems ok."

I breathed again. The acid test, passed. His voice dropped and he pointed to the sky. "Let's go inside. It isn't safe." He turned and stalked to his front door. Whether he meant it wasn't safe out here or in there, I wasn't sure, but I followed him in anyway.

He stood aside to let me pass into the hallway. His house had the same setup as all the rest of ours. Front door, living room off to the left. The hall went straight down the length of the house, opening on the right to two bedrooms, and on the left to the kitchen, which was open to the living room, and to the bathroom/laundry room at the end of the hall. It was a perfect rectangle. And Fox's was covered in newsprint.

At first I wasn't sure if it was wallpaper or not; it certainly covered all available vertical surfaces. But then I noticed that every page, every article had notations on it. Words circled or crossed out. Individual letters highlighted with lines bridging them, as if the last 20 years of news was nothing more than his own personal Word Search.

The sound of locks clicking behind me broke me from my thoughts. Fox clicked, switched, turned, bolted, and chained a line of locks down the door, plucked a hair from his head, and slipped it into the door frame. He leaned back, satisfied. With a quick turn, he whisked past me, clapping me on the back as he went. He disappeared into the kitchen.

I waited at the door, unsure of what I was supposed to do. I had seen *A Beautiful Mind*, and the reality of someone living like this made my mission less fun, and the letters I'd read and laughed about earlier this week seem almost cruel.

I set the letter down by the door and turned to the locks, hoping I could undo them all before he noticed I was escaping. But to no avail. Fox popped his head out of the kitchen and yelled, "Sugar?" I nodded, and he gestured with his hand for me to come in.

Walking down the hallway, I noticed a thin bulge underneath the newspapers. It was roughly shoulder height and looked like a picture frame that had been papered over. I wondered what it was, and if Fox remembered it was there. With my luck, it was probably *Transient Sunlight*. Before I could look, Fox reappeared out of the kitchen and handed me a mug. He wandered past me back down to the living room.

"Mr. Fox?" I entered the living room to find him sitting on a couch. He had removed the cushions and set them up around him like a house of cards. His own little fort. He looked at me questioningly as he raised his cup to his lips. I continued, "There's a picture on the wall in the hallway, but it's covered over with newspapers. Did you mean to do that?"

Fox muttered some words I couldn't hear, and when I repeated the question, he spoke again. "It was an accident. Forget it."

I sat on the floor and stared into my cup. It was filled with dry sugar. I looked up at Fox just as he was taking another sip. He crunched a few time, then his eyes focused on me.

"I didn't tell you to collect my mail." His eyes suddenly looked sad. "Why do you have my mail?"

I didn't know how to answer his question. I was distracted by the sudden changes in his mood, his voice, and his behaviour. Suddenly I pitied him. If it was distracting to see, how much more distracting was it to live?

I cleared my throat. "You know Mr. Fox, if you need help, there are lots of agencies that can—"

"Agencies!" Fox burst through the cushions like a submarine breaching the surface. "Don't tell me about agencies! I've had it up to here with agencies! Digging around asking questions. Questions questions always questions. Digging for answers where there aren't any answers just questions who and why always why why God questions without answers..."

Fox's voice trailed off and he sank onto the floor across from me, hugging his knees to his chest and rocking gently. I'd seen enough to both scare me and motivate me. I slowly rose, but his eyes didn't follow me. His lips kept mouthing the same words over and over again. I made my way quietly to the hallway and unlocked the door, one bolt at a time. It opened smoothly, and I had almost stepped outside when something made me change my mind. Quickly, I padded back down the hallway and lifted up the newsprint that hung over the frame. Without looking at it I snapped a picture with my cell phone camera, and turned back to the door.

As I passed the living room Fox's voice startled me. It was cold, and deep, and far more controlled.

"I figured out the agencies, you know. All those questions. Always wondering, always looking. Well, they can't look now." Fox started to croak out the same tune he had sung in his yard. *"All the day and all the night, all they see is shining light."* His eyes turned to follow me as I walked out the door and past the mirrors.

The mirrors Fox used to blind the satellites.

I sat on my couch that night, mulling over the picture that shone at me from my laptop screen. It was the photo I had taken in 1A.

It was Fox's family.

It was a classic family shot, taken on vacation at the Grand Canyon. A short blond woman with bright blue eyes stood at the back, looking weary but happy, one hand resting on her son's shoulder, the other pressing lightly on her belly, which was showing the first swellings of pregnancy. In front of her were a boy and a girl, both with black hair. Fox's daughter was tugging at the hem of her dress, trying in vain to keep the Arizona wind from sweeping it up around her waist. Her smile was genuine, but her brow was furrowed with the intense look of a strong-willed child at war with nature. The boy, who looked about eight years old, had a mischievous glint in his eye. You could just tell that for the last few moments he'd been driving his mother crazy by looking in every direction except at the camera. Wedged in behind his son and beside his wife was Fox. Fox's right leg was caught sticking out between his son and the fence behind him. He hadn't quite made it into position before the timer on the camera went. The vista spread behind them, an even split of earthy orange and endless blue.

A time worth remembering.

I was in research mode. When was this taken? Where was his family now? The large, chunky glasses on Fox's face said late 80s-early 90s. So did the neon purple fleece vest that his wife was wearing. But it was Fox's shirt that gave me the most information.

World's Greatest Dad - 1991.

That's what the shirt said. Emblazoned in bright green and orange across his chest, with a picture underneath. I zoomed in. It was a grainy photo of his children, taken some years before the trip to Arizona. They were smiling unending gap-toothed grins and holding up a piece of cardboard. On it, written in thick black marker and puff paint were the words:

We love you Daddy!
Love from
Jeffery & Alison.

I set my laptop aside. I had names and dates. I should be able to find out something about Fox's family.

I had just made up my mind to put the mystery aside for the night and get some sleep when there was a tap at my front door.

Not a knock. A tap.

I got up and shifted the blinds of my front window. Standing directly in front of the window, glaring into my eyes with only the glass and an inch of air between us was Sylvia. She jerked her finger towards the door and arched her right eyebrow. Her meaning was clear.

Open.

Now.

I did as directed, and was immediately joined in my doorframe by my guest. She crowded in, towering over me and cleared her throat.

"There's no such thing as a free lunch. Get your coat. We have work to do." Sylvia turned briskly back into the night and walked straight out to the street without waiting to see if I was following along.

I followed along.

I scurried past Noah's unit, out through the gates, and onto the sidewalk. Idling in front of the wall, lit only by the two small spotlights that illuminated the wooden "Stony Creek Estates" sign was a 1967 Ford Country Squire station wagon. It boasted a sky blue paint job and imitation wood panelling along the sides.

Sylvia had already climbed in the passenger seat, and Louise was hurriedly gesturing to the seat behind her. I whipped around the car and climbed in, buckling myself into the middle seat so I could see between them. In spite of the roomy interior, both Louise and Sylvia's heads brushed the ceiling of the car and they filled the front seats from side to side and back to front. Sylvia even managed to look cramped. But then again, her face always had that slightly displeased look.

Louise put the car in gear and pressed her foot gently on the gas. We eased out into non-existent traffic carefully, each of us swivelling our heads and calling out "all clear on this side!"

After crawling down a few streets, cautiously keeping an eye out for pedestrians, other cars, bicyclists, fallen trees, and runaway baby carriages, we reached the highway and Louise sped up to a leisurely 50 kph.

Other drivers flew past us on our right, honking and yelling abuse. Louise gave each one of them a smile and a slight nod of her head to indicate she had received their complaints and would make sure that someone in management would get back to them.

Sylvia, it seemed, was management, and freely returned insults and hand gestures with the fluent delivery of a native speaker.

I dared an interruption. "Where are we going?"

Louise glanced at me in the rear-view. "Oh, Sylvia didn't tell you?"

I shook my head. She turned her eyes on her sister, reproachfully. Sylvia sighed and shifted around to face me.

"We're going to jail." She turned back to the front and smiled. Louise snorted and eased off the gas. I turned and watched a cyclist pass us in the bike lane. He flashed a grin and gave me a thumbs-up. Sylvia cheerfully flipped him off.

He left us in the dust.

During the 45 minute drive I got the whole story out of the sisters. It turned out that one of the inmates they corresponded with was considering whether or not to tell them where he had hidden the money he had "liberated." If he did, they would promise to invest it for him, and he would allow them to keep an agreed-upon percentage. Sylvia explained all of this rather dryly; it was a deal they clearly had made many times before.

We pulled into the prison parking lot. The sisters marched together up to the front door as if they owned the place, and I followed meekly behind. At the front desk Sylvia stepped forward and claimed our visitor badges from a pair of guards. One of the guards, who had the name *George* embroidered on his uniform, had often seen both of the sisters before and greeted them by name. The other, a younger man, gaped up at them.

Both of the Gordon sisters were wearing dark jeans and black turtlenecks that accentuated their height. Their heads were severely charged with static electricity from rubbing against the ceiling of the car and their hair was sticking out in all directions. They looked like a pair of giant sparklers come to life.

Sylvia gave the younger man a firm look, and George told him to be polite, and buzzed us through to the visitor's room. I sat on a bench by the wall and wiped the sweat from my palms as Louise and Sylvia pleasantly chatted with the guard assigned to our meeting, whom they referred to as Tom, and seated themselves at a table.

We didn't have to wait long for our inmate to arrive. He was ushered in by yet another guard who placed him in his chair across from our party and, nodding to Tom, left us to our business. The spiky-haired inmate took his time arranging himself in his chair and looking us over. I don't know what he thought of us, but I know we were quite a sight; two Amazons that looked like they'd just stepped out of a light socket and me, trembling against the wall, willing my hands not to shake over the notepad that Louise had handed to me on our way in.

I felt as though I should have given myself a mild electrocution, just so I could fit in.

The inmate leaned in. His voice was low and gravelly. "You're the Gordon Sisters? I've heard about you from... you know... friends." With this he fell silent and glanced over his shoulder at the guard.

Louise leaped into the gap. "Oh, don't worry about Tom. That's all taken care of." She nodded to the guard and he took a deep breath and began to sing a lusty version of *I am a Pirate King*.

Sylvia leaned in and redirected the con's attention. "You've heard of us? It's all true, I can guarantee it."

Louise nodded and they proceeded to bounce the ball of conversation between one another, pausing only for breath.

"We've worked with many of your... *friends* before—"

"To our mutual advantage—"

"And have decided that your current situation—"

"Requires exactly the kind of delicacy that we provide."

"The *feminine* delicacy."

Sylvia shot a look over to me. "Discretion is our watchword."

I gulped.

The inmate's eyes were wide. He'd obviously heard about these two women, but hadn't really believed it to be true. Hell, I was a full-fledged partner, and I didn't believe it. Tom's warbling baritone filled the room, *"But I'll be true to the song I sing, and live and die... a Pirate King!"*

The prisoner opened his mouth, but the sisters didn't give him a chance to speak.

"Our fee is standard."

"20 percent."

"Which is a better deal than you'll get from the Fellini brothers—"

"Or from the Peruvian Banker—"

"And it is non-negotiable. So there are just two questions."

"How much was it?"

"And where is it now?"

Both Louise and Sylvia fell back in their chairs, eyebrows arched, sales pitch complete. The inmate closed his mouth and rubbed his chin. Tom quieted and stared at the wall above the sisters' heads. I sat up, pencil poised over the notepad.

The inmate blinked rapidly. He shook his head and nodded to himself. He leaned forward slowly, and everyone else in the room followed suit, except for Tom, who seemed to be intently counting the ceiling tiles. At a sign from Louise, he began to sing again.

"I am the very model of a modern major general..."

The prisoner spoke in a hushed tone. "2.5 million dollars, cash. Behind the bedroom wall, apartment 37, 128 View St. I was working for this bank—"

Louise interrupted him, "We don't need to know the hows and whys. All that's left is this; —"

Sylvia flowed in with the information, "The money will be kept for you under a false name at a bank of our choosing."

"Upon the date of your release, we will contact you—"

"And present you with the bank name, branch number, client name, and account number."

"All that will remain is for you to close the account."

The sisters stood up and shook his hand one at a time. Then, without a word to the con, Tom, or me, they swept out of the room side-by-side.

I turned to the inmate who was still sitting with his mouth open, unsure of what he had done. Tom cut off his song mid-phrase and stepped forward, placing his hand on the man's shoulder.

The inmate started and looked up at me. I swallowed.

"It's been a pleasure doing business with you." I said, as nonchalantly as possible. He closed his mouth and I turned to the door, trying desperately to imitate the sisters' self-possession. As Tom turned him towards the door that led back to his cell I tossed one final remark over my shoulder.

"We'll be in touch."

I caught up with Louise and Sylvia in the lobby as they handed their passes back to George. I tossed mine on the counter and followed them outside, walking as calmly as I could. 2.5 million dollars. And only four people in the world knew where it was. My mind was filled with thoughts of bikini-clad girls on private yachts, touring the Mediterranean.

Sylvia snapped me from my reverie. She was walking calmly in front of me towards the car, but her hand was waving freakishly down by her side, demanding my attention. I caught up to them and walked along beside.

"Did you write it down? The address?"

I nodded. "It's right here—"

"Well, don't wave it around so everyone can see it!" she snapped. I scanned the empty parking lot and bit my tongue.

"Oh, it's fine," soothed Louise. "Now memorize it."

We got to the car and climbed in. I scanned the words I'd scribbled on the paper and repeated them over and over in my head. *Apartment 37, 128 View St. Apartment 37, 128 View St. Apartment 37, 128 View St. Behind the bedroom wall.*

"I've got it," I announced as Louise pulled the car smoothly out of the parking lot and began to follow the drive back to the highway. Sylvia turned on the radio. Billy Joel informed us that he didn't start the fire.

"Say it." Sylvia didn't trust me yet, but I was working on it. After all, I was an accomplice now. I repeated the address three times. She made the camel sound and turned away from me.

[56]

"That's good," said Louise. "Now get rid of it."

I pondered that for a moment. I couldn't throw it out the window. Someone could find it, plus that would be littering. Which, as I thought about it, didn't seem that big of a deal compared with being an accessory after the fact and withholding evidence. I pulled open the ashtray that was built into the console between the sisters' seats, but a noise from Sylvia made me change my mind. I searched the car for a better solution, but none presented itself.

Oh well.

I stuffed the paper in my mouth and started to chew. Sylvia didn't turn her head, but I saw her cheeks lift in a smile just as we hit the highway.

Louise floored it.

I was thrown back into my seat, choking on the wad of paper as Louise weaved us in and out of traffic, narrowly missing slower vehicles. We flashed past a soccer mom's minivan and a trophy wife's convertible and shot into the middle lane.

Louise's face was a mask of concentration, and she didn't blink or breathe except when Sylvia reminded her by lightly tapped her arm with her left hand. Sylvia's right hand was firmly gripping the door handle, which made her look as if she were prepared to dive from the car at a moment's notice. I leaned forward, bracing myself on the seatbacks in front of me with my knees and placing my arms up against the ceiling. I could feel the hair on my arms rising as they reacted to the static electricity. Or maybe that was fear.

Louise bellowed, "To the right?" as a moving truck ahead of us began to brake in anticipation of a yellow light.

Sylvia responded through her clenched teeth, "All clear."

The station wagon jerked right, grazing the truck's mud-flap, and flew through the intersection. I looked behind us in time to catch the look of astonishment on the driver's face, and then he was swallowed up by the blur of the hurried past.

"Jordan, you're on cop-watch!" Louise tried to squeeze out a smile as she said it, but was distracted by a jaywalking pedestrian. She stomped on the brakes and brought us to an abrupt stop in the middle of the highway. I joined both sisters in glaring at the shaken teenager as she stumbled back onto the shoulder.

Sylvia double-tapped Louise's arm.

I looked ahead and belatedly sputtered, "Cop."

A patrol car was stopped at the upcoming intersection, but the occupants weren't looking our way. Sylvia turned to look at me with wry amusement.

"Thanks Jordan. Now I see why we brought you." I blushed and shrugged and Louise carefully drove through the intersection, laboriously obeying every traffic law.

"Why were we speeding?" I asked aloud, guessing that this break wouldn't be for long. "Won't that... I dunno, draw attention we don't want?"

Sylvia glanced at Louise. Louise shrugged and said, "It's a risk we have to take. Sooner or later *they'll* come for the money too, and we need to get there first." She obviously felt there was no need for her to clarify who *they* were.

"But, I thought you said Tom wouldn't say anything."

"Oh, Tom won't." Sylvia answered while Louise performed a neck-wrenching shoulder check and turned us into the downtown core. "But we got a tip that they might have recorded our conversation tonight. It's a bit suspicious you know, us seeing all those prisoners."

I bit my tongue again. *You think?*

Louise turned on her signal light and remained in the centre lane for a full thirty seconds before sliding over. "By the way Sylvia, getting Tom to sing was a great idea. I hope he doesn't get into trouble."

"Oh, Tom can handle things."

I returned to the topic foremost in my mind. "But then, can't you get arrested, if they know you know the hiding place?"

"Only if they find us in possession of the articles." Sylvia had obviously studied this in detail. "Or if they find us at the scene, breaking into the walls."

Louise pulled the car to a stop behind a building and put it in park. "And that's why we hurry." She unbuckled her seatbelt and opened the door. She and Sylvia walked up to the front door of the building and started pushing random buzzers. Sylvia turned back to me as I got out of the car.

"Oh, and Jordan. Don't forget the sledgehammer."

No less than three of the residents at 128 View Street buzzed us in upon hearing Louise apologetically complain on conference call that she had left her keys in her apartment. I held the door open as they both trooped in wearing very satisfied smiles. We entered the elevator and I pressed the button for the third floor. We each put on a pair of medical gloves. No one said a word while we ascended, but a duet version of *The Girl from Ipanema* was playing through the speakers. Harp and pan flute. Its tinny warbling reflected the butterflies in my stomach. I tried to imagine it being played on Henry's stereo and felt braver.

We arrived at the door of apartment 37 and Louise nimbly picked the lock while Sylvia blocked the view of any curious neighbours and I tried to keep the sledgehammer out of sight. I started to whistle, but was given a look by both sisters and swallowed the tune.

"Got it." Louise swung the door open and we all three stepped inside. I closed the door behind us and turned just as Sylvia hit the lights.

The apartment was occupied.

At least, it was furnished. There was no sign of anyone there at the moment, but someone was currently living there. The IKEA catalogue collection was carefully placed around the room, in what I was sure was a young woman's attempt at making their place seem less student-ish. It achieved quite the opposite effect. The distinctive furniture style and art-nouveau lighting fixtures practically screamed low-budget. But at least it was empty.

I breathed a sigh of relief and heard it echoed twice from each sister. I realized then that they hadn't been sure of what to expect here either. I kicked myself mentally for not even considering the possibility that someone might have been home.

As we stole through the apartment I was amazed at how women so big could be so quiet. We whispered down the hall and into the only bedroom. I flicked on the lights and belatedly thought of another problem.

Behind the bedroom wall.

It had taken me this long to remember that a room generally has four walls.

I stood in the centre of the room, picturing myself bashing away at walls until the entire building collapsed around me. I could see myself surrounded by floating dust, watching two giantesses fling huge chunks of debris around, one to the left and one to the right, until the whole building was in two enormous piles around us, one labelled Alcatraz and the other labelled Sing Sing.

I needn't have worried. The sisters had no such intentions.

"That one." They spoke at the same time, a duet of certainty as they pointed towards the wall immediately beside the door.

I hesitated to ask. "How do you know?"

Sylvia grunted. "It won't be either of the outside walls—"

"The window takes up too much space," Louise provided the reasoning.

"And it won't be the closet wall—"

"Same reason."

"So it must be the door wall." I finished the logical process triumphantly. Sylvia nodded and grunted. I took a shot. "Plus, it's interior, so they could work on it without anyone outside being the wiser."

Louise clapped her hands in delight. "Oh, he's got it now! I knew there would be more than one use for you!"

Before I could ask her what she meant, Sylvia stepped behind me and pushed me towards the wall.

"Alright, Moriarty. Quietly."

Each swing punched a ragged hole into the wall, breaking the drywall into crumbly bits of dust. Every now and then the wall would catch the head of the hammer as if trying to put a stop to the violent destruction. Sylvia breathed through her shirt, her black hair picking up drywall dust that aged her considerably. Louise was in the living room where she had found the owner's stereo and put in a Journey CD, cranking the bass up to cover our misdeeds. She danced her way into the kitchen and poured us each a glass of water.

It was as she came back into the room that the sledgehammer hit something soft behind the wall. I stopped short at the unexpected feeling and glanced back at the sisters. Sylvia bounded off the bed and brushed me aside. She dug her arm into the hole in the wall, grasped something, and pulled. Her hand emerged clutching the dirty corner of an old grocery bag. The sisters exchanged a significant look. Sylvia turned to me.

"Good. Now, faster."

I turned back to the wall. The soundtrack of the evening's festivities filled my ears. I had become an accomplice to Gilbert & Sullivan, driven recklessly with Billy Joel, broken and entered with muzak, and now, in time to the beating of my heart, I was wilfully destroying private property to *Don't Stop Believing*.

I came to the conclusion that living on your own can lead to the creation of some awfully strange mix-tapes.

2.5 million dollars is a lot of money. About 25 kilograms, when it's all in nicely stacked $100 bills, which this was.

I had pulled the last package from the wall. The money had been in four small bags, which I thought wasn't very much. If this had been a Hollywood movie, I'm sure we'd have had to take at least seven huge bags out of the wall, and probably dumped them out on the bed and rolled around in the pile of bills. As it was, I was a little disappointed.

All told, the money was piled into ten stacks, each just over a foot high. Sylvia and Louise carefully placed the money into a selection of backpacks brought especially for the occasion. I wandered over to the window and peered out at the darkened street below.

My breath caught in my throat. I forced it out, and it carried a single word with it.

"Cops."

I pressed up against the window. Louise hurried up beside me and looked out. The street was empty save for a single patrol car slowly cruising down the street. I could see the officer's face as she gazed up at the building and spoke into her radio.

Louise turned briskly back to Sylvia, who had just finished packing up the money. "Patrol unit. It's not an invasion, but we shouldn't stick around."

Sylvia flung a backpack over her shoulder and stood up. "Time to go." Louise grabbed another pack and they left me standing in the semi-destroyed bedroom with two bags full of money and a sledgehammer. I could hear them shuffling down the hall beside each other, flicking off light switches as they went.

"Coming, Jordan? Or would you prefer to stay here and wait for the police?" Sylvia's voice rang down the hallway. I heard the front door unbolt and came to my senses. I whipped around the corner and hurried to the door.

"Sorry to keep you waiting." I smiled sweetly past Sylvia's frown. "Didn't want to leave our DNA on these for the cops to find." I held up the three glasses I had snatched from the bedroom floor on my way out.

Louise tried to hide her smile behind her hand. Sylvia glowered and muttered that I watched too much CSI. I held my head high and refused to meet her glare as we turned the corner and took the stairs back down to the lobby.

I stepped into my unit and closed the door. The rest of the evening had been uneventful, comparatively. Sylvia and I had taken the bags down to the garage level and waited there in what I'm sure she'd meant to be an uncomfortable silence while Louise got the car and came around to the back to pick us up. I had loaded the wagon and we'd piled in, Louise carefully turning us back out onto the street.

As we'd driven round the corner, out of sight of the building, I had looked back and seen the flashes of light that meant our patroller had just become a first response unit. We'd gotten out just in time.

I stood now in the hallway of my unit and pondered the evening's events. It wasn't until now that I'd had time to think about the morality of what I was getting involved in. I slumped onto the couch and tallied up my sins and virtues.

One: Was it even stealing? Technically, the money had been given to us by the previous caretaker, so I hadn't stolen anything, except for the three glasses, which had been thrown into a recycling bin on the way home.

Two: I suppose the money had been stolen once before, but I assumed that the original owners had been recompensed by insurance, so that wasn't an issue for me.

Three: As for the damage I'd done to the apartment wall, Sylvia had made sure to leave a few bills behind that would cover any necessary repairs. The resident would have a new wall and Swedish-made bedroom set in no time. We had probably done them a favour by forcing the upgrade, at our expense.

In fact, the only point my conscience could prick me with was that we were going to give the money back to the original thief. But I noted that none of my share was going towards convicted felons. In fact, I could choose to spend my money in ways that would help other people, and that would redeem any moral deficiencies I had inherited through my actions.

Thus soothed, I stood and turned down the hallway towards my bedroom. My conscience was tired.

It had been a long week.

Saturday, August 23

I awoke to the sound of a light scratching on my door. It was 8:14 AM according to my alarm clock, which wisely remained silent as I stumbled out of bed and down the hall, peering into the morning light through half-opened eyes, very nearly losing a toe to a dimly-lit hat-rack. In a foul temper I swung open the door, prepared to berate whatever individual dared to wake me before I'd had my morning coffee.

There was no one there. Just a note and a cardboard tube.

I stared dumbly at the items for a full minute before remembering my state of undress and collected them into the house. I sat and tried to carefully open the note with fingers still blistered from last night's burglary. After a few seconds of fumbling, I got impatient and tore it. It read:

> JM,
>
> I have some business to attend to today outside of the walls of our little sanctuary. I was hoping you would be able to act as an agent for a sale I wanted to broker. The item in question I believe you are already familiar with. I offer, of course, the standard handling fee of 10%. The buyer will arrive at your door at 9:00 this morning. I assume you remember his name. Trusting the impertinence can be forgiven,
>
> SS

I slowly let the letter drop to the floor. How one small piece of paper could carry so much weight, I'd never know.

Sasha just assumed I'd do it. And of course, I was in no position to deny this, since the note also made it clear that she/he knew that I knew about his/her sales practices and that I'd been reading her/his mail. And to sweeten the deal, I'd be paid. Again. And the last sentence. Did Sasha want me to forgive the impertinence of asking me to get involved, or was it meant to imply that she/he would be willing to forgive my reading of his/her mail if I did as she/he asked?

I really needed a cup of coffee.

I had showered and dressed and I sat in the kitchen sipping away at a cup of Tim Hortons' blend. Sasha's map lay unrolled on the table before me. I stared down at it. I had taken some history in high school, but could not for the life of me remember a time when the USSR had officially denied the existence of Iceland. And yet, between the great grey mass of Greenland and the emerald-green empire of the British Isles, the Soviet cartographer had painted nothing but the pale blue of the Northern Atlantic.

Too bad for you, Reykjavik.

A knock sounded at the door. I rushed to open it, conscious that I was representing someone else's business interests. I paused with my hand on the knob and breathed deeply, squaring my shoulders and lifting my chin in an attempt to appear mysterious. Whoever Sasha Sterling was, their agent had an image to maintain.

The man at the door could almost have been Henry's twin. He was similarly short and studious-looking, with a soft voice and quiet manner. His one major difference was his sheer bulk. Where Henry was slight and sharp, Dr. Barnaby Hender was a mass of flesh. He entered at my invitation, quivering a plethora of chins that bobbled over a vertical track of straining buttons. The elbow patches of his tweed jacket were worn down, rubbed by the walls of the various hallways they had led him through as if they were the supports that kept his tremendous body from leaning too far in any direction, thus avoiding a horrible collapse. He entered the living room and sat down on the couch, enveloping it.

I brought the map forward and set it on the coffee table. He peered down at it through a pair of reading glasses that he'd rescued from his breast pocket and mashed onto his face. His voice was the dry, dusty mutter of the professional historian who spoke often of people, but rarely to them.

"Hmmm, China in red of course, but Panama in yellow? Peculiar, very peculiar. How much?"

Caught unawares by this last, which was directed towards me, I had a moment of panic. Sasha had never mentioned a price to me. Was I supposed to make up my own, or perhaps negotiate an amount with the good doctor? I decided to follow the path of least resistance.

Struggling to maintain my aloof facade, I said imperiously, "the price has not changed, Dr. Hender," praying that Sasha had already set one in a previous letter or perhaps in the ad itself.

Hender's eyes struggled to reach me through his heavy eyelids and when they did I caught an unexpected twinkle in them.

"And nor shall it, I presume?" He smiled, and his pleasant face became a rippling fabric of sagging jowls that were pinned like curtains to the corners of his mouth. "Well, it is the genuine article; anyone can see that, so I suppose I can't haggle with you."

He reached into his inside pocket, and I could almost hear the stitches of his jacket screaming in pain. "Here's the cheque. Certified, just like you requested. I have to say, although your methods of communication are... unusual, to say the least, it has been a pleasure doing business with you, Mr. Sterling."

He waved off my attempts to help him from the couch and rumbled out of the front door like a roly-poly Panzer. I closed the door behind him and watched my couch cushions re-inflate. The cheque in my hands was still moist from whatever secretions Dr. Hender had left on it, and I held it up between my thumb and forefinger to allow it to dry.

The doctor's spidery scrawl ran across the cheque in informative designs. Memo: 1962 "Operation Kalininsk" Soviet World Map. Pay to the Order of: Sasha Sterling. In the Amount of: $7,500.00.

I did the math. $750. Plus my cut of last night's take.

My alarm clock went off. It was 9:13.

So far, I liked university.

It was Saturday, so no mail was forthcoming. For the first time since arriving here last Monday, the day was mine. I decided to go to the hospital and visit Grace.

What with all the strange activity I'd been involved with over the last few days, I was ashamed to admit that I had completely forgotten my original intention of helping Noah. As I sat on the bus on my way to the hospital, I resolved to use some of my newfound wealth to help our grumpy complex manager. I was still unsure as to how I was going to do that, but I figured the answer would present itself at the proper moment. In the meantime, I stopped off at the gift shop and picked up a small pot of African violets to go with the present I'd brought Grace.

The nurse at the front desk gave me Grace's room number, and I fidgeted in the elevator, listening to John Tesh insert flowing arpeggios into *My Heart Will Go On*, and feeling a distinct sense of déjà vu. I got off on the 4th floor and promised myself that I wouldn't take a sledgehammer to anything in Grace's room.

At my hesitant knock, Grace's voice called me into the room, whistling into the hall with a clarity that belied the weakness her body displayed.

She lay in her bed, supported by pillows. The room looked very much like a hospital room. The starched linen matched the thin pillowcases which matched the wrinkled gown that Grace wore. The gleaming floors matched the plain walls which matched the sterile faces of the doctors as they padded back and forth down the hall, always busily going to someone else's room. Grace's thin frame was dwarfed by the hospital bed. But her weary expression changed to delight when she saw me enter the room, and the large pink bow that she wore in her hair shouted in defiance against the dead cleanliness of health.

"Jordan, dear! You are such a sweet boy to give up your vacation time to come visit an old heifer like me. Now don't you shake your head at me, I know what I am and I'm not ashamed of it, so I'm certainly not going to let you be ashamed of it. Are those flowers for me? How lovely, just go ahead and put them on the windowsill. Just a little to the left dear, so they'll catch the light. That's just right."

Grace halted her monologue momentarily to admire the violets. "They seem to affect the whole room, don't they dear? As if they're giving the sunlight the warmth and colour it needs to cheer up this drab old room and the drab old woman in it. Oh, now I've shocked you again. Well, you'll have to get used to it, I'm afraid. The doctors say I'm not going anywhere anytime soon. Just the same old ticker, missing a beat every now and then. Is it terrible of me to hope I kick the bucket this very minute, if only to prove them wrong? The one thing that will change as you age, dear, is that you discover that where you used to dislike doctors being wrong, you now dislike it when they're right. Is that for me too?"

She pointed at the package under my arm, the gift I had brought from home. I leaned forward and deposited it beside her fragile body. Grace tore into the wrapping like a five-year old at Christmas, revealing the lumpy, broken hedgehog that had been damaged on the night of her removal to the hospital.

"I tried to glue it all back together, but I think I put some of the spines on the wrong way..." I trailed off, my feeble explanation hardly covering the new punk look that Grace's hedgehog sported.

"Don't be silly dear, it's perfect," Grace said kindly. She held the figurine up and spoke to it, nose to nose. "Much better than you were. A common catalogue creation no longer, isn't that right Wilfred? And looking so fearsome, too. I'll bet that mean old Patton won't bother you anymore. Why, you're right as rain."

I gently took Wilfred from her hands, which were starting to shake with the strain of holding him up. Setting him on the windowsill next to the flowerpots, I took advantage of the break in Grace's speech.

"I can't imagine Patton ever bothering anyone. It looks to me like he just sits around all day."

"Don't let that old bully fool you. He's always had it in his mind that he owns the whole complex, and anything in it is his to do with as he pleases." Her eyes glinted with a mischievous spark. "And that goes for his dog too."

I laughed at her interpretation of Noah's gruffness. "I wonder if the real Patton would be impressed by that dog's behaviour."

"To hear Noah tell of him, absolutely not. He always talks of General Patton as if the man were a god." Grace's voice descended an octave in a loose imitation of Noah's gravelly manner. "Decision, action, and consequences, that was his way, and if it was good enough for George S. Patton, then it's good enough for me, dammit!"

Grace lay back on her pillows, smiling at me. Her usual briskness wouldn't normally allow for much give-and-take in a conversation, but her weakness willed it.

I didn't mind. I could do small talk today.

"That sounds just like him. I'll bet he sounded like that when he was just a kid, too."

The smile faded from Grace's face and her eyes drooped, heavy with sudden memories. "No, he wasn't always like that. Or at least, he was less like it." A stray lock of white hair fell from behind her ear. She brushed it back with a shaky hand and visibly rebounded. "Now of course, he's just another grumpy old man, with plenty of complaints to make and not a thing to complain about."

I sat back in my chair and looked at the violets. The late afternoon sun shone through them and their shadow filled the room. I thought of the letter that Noah had been sent from the Korea Veterans Association of Canada. It seemed to me that a man with his history had the right to complain. But I deferred to Grace's expertise. It was something in the way she spoke that made me think she knew more than she was telling.

Grace was looking at the violets too. I watched her eyes as they followed the edge of sunlight along the shadow of the flowers, down the wall and across the floor where it climbed up her bed and stretched cosily over her legs like an old cat. Her thoughts must have mirrored mine because she spoke quietly, "The war was a terrible time for him, of course. A terrible time for so many. And we all had to live with it, even us at home."

Her eyes turned to me and I saw the glint of comfortable tears in them. "I had a brother who fought in Korea, you know. He was a brave boy. Looked a bit like you, only taller and more handsome. No offence, dear."

I waved away her apology. She turned back towards the window.

"He never came home. I think if he had, he may have wished he hadn't. At least he died a hero. At least he didn't have to live with his own memories and his nation's forgetfulness. That would have been hard for Bill. He was very... memorable."

Grace fell silent, and for the first time since I met her I realized I saw her not as Grandma Grace, but as a real person. It frightened me. Suddenly I didn't want to be in this hospital, sharing her memories, her grief and her fear. I felt the full weight of relationship and found it unbearable.

I rose to leave.

Grace returned to herself with a bright post script.

"Just one thing before you go, dear. If I can ask. I'll probably be getting a piece of mail from the university within the next few days. Proofreading. A teacher can never retire they say. Those who can't do, teach, and those who can't teach anymore, teach anyway. I wonder, could you bring it by if you're not too busy? It'll be delivered right to your door. You can help *me* that way you know. Just like you're helping the others." It was the first time she had referenced the message she gave me the night the ambulance came. The certainty with which she said it made me feel guilty.

She continued, "I don't want to be a bother but... oh why pretend. Of course I want to be a bother. I want you to bring it to me, and stay to visit. No one else comes by but the dreadful doctors and the nurses, who are sweet enough in their way but still can't manage to disguise the fact that their entire existence is centred around poking, prodding, and pinching an old woman who has no desire to be poked, prodded, or pinched any more than they do. Say you'll bring it by; if you do, I'll make you some more cookies just as soon as they let me out. Thank you, Jordan. You *are* a dear."

This final monologue seemed to empty Grace completely, and she sank back into her pillows looking frailer than when I had arrived. I promised to bring her any essays that might appear and something frivolous to help her pass the time. We said our goodbyes and I backed quietly out of the door. I remained silent for the entire journey home, remembering that I had told my dad that what I wanted most out of university was to meet a different kind of people. Real people.

Real people hurt, sometimes.

When I got back to Stony Creek, I found a cheque from Sasha for $750 in an envelope under the mat. I dropped it on the kitchen table and headed back out the door, making a point of delivering the coupons I had cut out for my neighbours and Henry's chess letter from Argentina.

He was thrilled to have it and brought me inside to watch him move the piece. It was the bronze set they were playing on. The plastic set still stood unused. Henry saw me eyeing it and rushed into the kitchen to scribble something on a piece of paper.

I wandered across the living room and stared upwards at the speakers. On the floor to my left was one of Henry's CDs, unpackaged and sturdily keeping a mug of coffee from spilling onto the floor. I shook my head. I had just listened to his music the night he gave it to me, before I went to bed.

It was astonishing. And he was using it as a coaster. I shook my head again.

Henry appeared at my side with an envelope. It had my name on it. "What's this?"

"It's a letter. For you. You'll see when you open it, only don't open it *untilYOUGETHOME!!*" His voice rose in a crescendo as he saw my fingers teasing at the envelope flap. I swore up and down that I wouldn't dream of opening it any earlier than when I stepped into my unit, fifteen metres away. He smiled triumphantly and edged me towards the door.

A thought struck me; a way to kill two birds with one stone, and I paused.

"An addendum," I said, "to that promise. I'll keep it if you give me another one of your CDs."

Henry goggled.

"It's a gift," I explained. "I know someone who will love it."

He obliged with fervour only gracious pride can elicit, and sent me on my way.

Grace needed something to cheer up her time in the hospital. I figured that Henry's voice might just be able to sing the life back into her.

I opened the envelope as soon as I stepped in the door.
Opening. Pawn to e4.
I was officially playing chess with a Grand Master.

Sunday, August 24

It was Sunday morning, so I had decided to turn off my alarm clock. A knock on the door woke me promptly at 7:30. It was a right-leaning Louise.

"Oh, look at you. Slug-a-bed. Well, you can go back to sleep in a minute. This is for you." She leaned in conspiratorially and handed me an envelope. "Your cut. Even Sylvia agrees that you earned it, bashing in the walls and spotting the police."

It crossed my mind that there was no bank in the world that would accept a deposit of 2.5 million dollars without asking questions. I looked up at Louise.

"How...? What bank...? It's not possible," I finished lamely.

Louise laughed at my naivety and spoke in a low whisper, "Anything is possible."

I wanted to ask more, but as the envelope lay in my hand and I felt the weight of possibility inside it, I figured mine was not to reason why. I closed my fingers around it eagerly.

Louise lifted her left eyebrow. "Maybe you have a girl to spend it on?" My eyes darted over her shoulder towards Jenny's house. Louise didn't notice, and took my silence for bashful virginity. She marched back to her house, her laugh sounding strangely like a lonely harmony line. I decided I preferred the two sisters together. Without Sylvia, Louise was oddly forward. Without Louise, Sylvia could be disturbingly polite. Together, they were as they should be. Themselves, and nothing less.

I almost didn't want to look at the cheque in my hand. I felt the same sensation I feel when I'm reading an exciting book and I know I'm coming to a cliff-hanger chapter ending. I always want to flip my eyes over to the final sentence to find out what happens, but I know that I shouldn't. Sweet, excruciating anticipation.

We'd never officially settled on my cut. I knew that the sisters took 20 percent of the total amount, which in this case would come to 500,000 dollars. What my cut of that was, I had no idea. I walked calmly back to my bedroom and climbed into bed, burying my head under the covers.

I held the cheque against my chest. Even one percent would be 5000 dollars.

I couldn't wait any longer. I flipped back the covers and looked at the amount.

$50,000.00

Ten percent.

I wanted to run up and down the hallway and scream. I wanted to tear the cheque up and race to confession. I wanted to pound on their door and demand to know how they could so trust someone they had hardly met.

But I didn't do any of those things.

I just pulled the covers back over my head.

After all, it was Sunday morning. A certain decorum had to be maintained.

I spent most of the day in a sort of meditative state, floating through the rooms of my house, unable to see distinct futures due to the haze of possibilities, mentally sifting through my options. This time, I remembered the promise to myself.

Help Noah.

But I didn't want to limit myself there. This was the first time in my life that I was in a position to do anything for anybody. Grace had reawakened my drive in the hospital.

I stood in front of *Transient Sunlight*. Underneath were all the pages of information I had collected on my neighbours. I didn't want to look at them. They seemed an insult to the people I had been getting to know.

Mere facts, inconclusive and impersonal. Grace's life could not be summed up with words. Fox's couldn't be explained in point form. Henry's couldn't even be described in a single language.

I took down the picture. The facts stared at me from the wall, a naive teenager's idea of research. My study had brought me more than I had bargained for, and I now found myself going native, like so many researchers before me who found their subjects to be more than just fodder for another article.

I tore the sheets down, and replaced them with a single piece of paper. I would make a list. A list of ideas.

I had 50,000 dollars of morally indefensible money, and one week until school started. I would use them to better the lives of my neighbours.

As I began scribbling ideas onto the wall, I had the funny feeling that my father would be proud of me.

Monday, August 25

My alarm clock went off at 6:30, 6:45, and 7:00 AM. I calmly sat up in bed, reached over, and unplugged it. The beeping was cut off mid-shriek.

I smiled.

I wandered through the kitchen into the living room, picking up a croissant on the way. I stopped at *Transient Sunlight* and pictured the list behind it. I smiled again.

This was going to be the best Monday ever.

I heard a noise outside my door. A rustling of paper. My eyes shot to the front hallway.

Could it be?

This entire last week I'd been unable to figure out the mail carrier's schedule; they always seemed to have delivered it before I awoke, even if I was up at 4:30 AM. I hustled to the door and whipped it open, hoping to catch by surprise the one man responsible for the events of the last seven days.

Sitting in the plastic chair to my right, flipping through a pile of mail, was a police officer.

I froze in the doorway, suddenly physically aware of my place in the world. I could measure the exact distance to my coffee table, where sat a cheque for $50,000. I could feel the change in mass of Sasha's body as the kidney was removed, and Sasha's bank account as the $150,000 was deposited. I recalled the various speeds of Louise's getaway car and the humidity of my kitchen as the steam flouted the law, one envelope at a time.

All this I felt before the officer looked up from the mail and met my eyes. They were sunken deeply into his gaunt face.

"Jordan, right?" I think I nodded.

"Inspector Paul Longstaff, VicPD." He reached out and shook my hand. I noticed he was still holding the pile of mail. "May I come in for a minute?"

Over his shoulder I saw Louise and Sylvia at the window of their unit. Louise looked worried and Sylvia glared out at me, raising one finger in silent warning. *Don't squeal.*

I shook my head and gathered my wits. "I'd prefer it if you didn't, sir. It's a real mess."

Longstaff had already taken a step towards the door before I'd answered, assuming entry. He stopped, surprised when I didn't move from the doorway and we ended up nose to nose. I noticed that although his face was drawn and pale, it still held a dry humour and a watchful eye. He'd caught the flicker of my eyes and slowly turned towards the sisters' house, but all that was there was a rippling curtain. He turned back towards me.

"No problem, let's just chat out here then." He ambled over to the dry fountain and sat on the rim. He patted the space next to him.

I slowly made my way out to the centre of the courtyard, fully conscious that my boxers had a large Superman "S" emblazoned on the front. I remembered reading a mystery novel once where the lead detective had employed the tactic of making his suspect as uncomfortable as possible during interrogation to make him spill the beans. I made up my mind that I wasn't going to be the rat. Ok, so maybe the cops were here, and maybe they were going to question me in public in nothing but my boxers. But they were, after all, *Superman* boxers.

I could withstand anything but kryptonite.

I sat down with what I hoped was an air of self-possession. Inspector Longstaff looked amusedly at my wardrobe, clicked his tongue and flipped open his notepad.

"So, your complex manager, Mr. Foster told me that you've just moved in. All set for school next week?"

Easy questions. He was softening me up. I responded with alacrity.

"Yes sir. Still trying to get my bearings. It's my first time on my own. Can I ask what this is about?" *I'll ask the questions here*, I thought.

The Inspector frowned slightly. He ignored my question. "Well, living alone for the first time. That's always exciting. Lots of new people to meet. New activities to try. Have you done anything interesting recently?"

I adopted a studious frown. "Well, I've started playing chess by mail." He glanced down at the mail in his hand. I realized that maybe I shouldn't have brought his attention to it. I hurried on, "and I've visited my elderly neighbour Grace in the hospital." *That should be worth some brownie points.*

Longstaff had stopped listening to me. Fox had just exited his house and was dragging what appeared to be a cannibalized satellite dish past his mirrors. He shuffled out of the gate and vanished around the corner. The Inspector's pen was poised over his notepad but he just stared at the gate, the afterimage of Fox's bright yellow raincoat burned into his retina.

Welcome to the jungle, Inspector, I thought. *You're on my turf now.*

He collected himself. "Interesting bunch of people you've got here, eh? Quite a collection." I followed his gaze around the courtyard, stopping to take in the Zen garden, Grace's wind-chimes, and the abandoned BBQ.

"You have no idea." As familiar as the sights and sounds of the complex had become to me, I was not so far removed that I couldn't sympathize with the Inspector's first impression.

"I wonder..." his voice trailed off. "Do any of your neighbours have any interesting habits?"

I stared at him. *All* of my neighbours had interesting habits.

He sighed and closed his notebook. "Look Jordan, I'm going to be straight with you. We got a tip that someone in this complex is involved in something... not strictly legal."

For someone being straight with me, Inspector Longstaff sure was beating around the bush. I feigned curiosity.

"I spoke to Mr. Foster, and he said you'd been interacting with everyone around here, and that you seemed like an upstanding young man."

I puffed out my chest with the pride of civic duty. Encouraged, Longstaff continued.

"I was hoping, that is, the department was hoping that you might help us out by keeping us informed if you see anything... suspicious." He cocked his eyebrow at me questioningly.

I responded with delight. "Sure, anything I can do! We'll all do our bit—"

He interrupted harshly, "No. No one else can know." His voice softened and he whispered conspiratorially, "I'm entrusting this mission to you. I know I can count on you, Superman."

Honestly, who did he think he was dealing with, a five-year old? I bobbed my head in eager agreement.

He stood and shook my hand again, then turned to leave. Fox re-entered the courtyard, saw a man in uniform walking towards him and yelped, sprinting at full speed into his house. I could hear the bolts slam into place from the fountain.

Longstaff paused and turned back to me. "That man, does he happen to own the blue station wagon parked out front?"

My heart skipped a beat. I shook my head. I could feel Sylvia's gaze burning into my back.

Inspector Longstaff stepped back towards me. "Does anyone else own it? Two women, perhaps?"

I could feel the sweat dripping off my forehead. So much for cool and collected. I shrugged nervously.

Longstaff took it all in and smiled. "Well, no matter. Thanks Jordan, you've been more helpful than you know. Don't forget to keep us informed; I'll be in touch."

Yeah, right. I wasn't going to tell him anything.

Longstaff smiled again, then looked down at his left hand in fake surprise. He was still holding the pile of mail. "That's right, I almost forgot. It seems as though you've been getting everyone's mail. I hope you're making sure that everyone gets what's coming to them." He passed the mail to me, holding on to it just a little longer then was comfortable, before turning on his heel and striding out the gate.

I stood in the middle of the courtyard in my Superman boxers.

Everyone gets what's coming to them.

That wasn't exactly subtle.

I went back inside.

No sooner had I thrown the mail onto the table then there were two knocks at the door. I closed my eyes.

"Come in Sylvia."

She barged round the corner and to my surprise, Louise followed her in. I had never had them both in my place at one time, and their size seemed to shrink the room. Louise sat on the couch with a worried expression. Sylvia made a wry face at *Transient Sunlight* and gestured that I should sit too.

"Well?" She tapped her finger on her forearm impatiently.

"He wants me to keep an eye on the people here. *Two sisters* especially. He's suspicious. And he knows about the station wagon. But I didn't say anything. I just nodded a lot."

Louise nodded in solidarity. Sylvia let out a breath. The camel sound. They looked at each other and spoke simultaneously.

"Goodman."

"Who's Goodman?" I demanded.

Louise piped up first. "Warden Harley Goodman runs the prison we went to Friday night."

Sylvia grabbed the baton of conversation. "He's been getting suspicious of us—"

"Of course, Tom doesn't tell him what we talk to the inmates about—"

"But over time, we think he's figured it out—"

"Until last week George (you remember George) told us he might have to tape our next interview."

I started to fill in the blanks. "But you had Tom sing so that he wouldn't hear what was being said." Sylvia preened for a moment. Having Tom sing had been her idea. I wondered momentarily how Tom had gotten away with that. He wasn't *that* good a singer.

Louise continued, "Unfortunately, he must have been able to hear the address somehow through the noise—"

I interrupted. "But then why did the cops just send a patroller to the apartment? Wouldn't they have just come to pick you up?" I asked. *And pick me up?*

"Hmmm... good point." Sylvia paced in front of the picture. "Unless..." She left the thought incomplete.

After a short pause Louise finished it. "Unless Goodman didn't give the tape to the police."

[79]

"That doesn't make any sense. You said he must have told them about the car. And to look out for two sisters." I was lost.

"But not our names—"

"Or they would have gone right to you, and not come to me?" I hazarded. Sylvia nodded. Her eyes narrowed.

"It all becomes clear. We seem to have found you at the perfect time, Jordan."

It was clear as mud to me, and I said so.

Louise shrugged. "Goodman must have tipped them off anonymously. They don't have any evidence, just suspicions—"

"So they'll just watch us and hope that we give ourselves away—"

"Or that I give you away." I realized I was slipping into the hand-me-down conversational stylings of the Gordon sisters.

Sylvia glared at me, hard. "But you won't."

"Oh, of course he won't Sylvia. Don't even say it." Louise got up from the couch and started towards the door. Sylvia was drawn along beside her and they stopped in the doorframe and turned, looking like a vertical pastry press in matching sweaters. I followed along at a safe distance.

"Keep us updated," Sylvia grunted again and the two sisters walked side-by-side back to their unit. I turned back into my house.

And saw Inspector Longstaff kneeling in front of Noah's unit, scribbling in his notebook. He caught my eye and held up the dog food coupon I'd placed there three days ago.

"Looks like a special delivery." He smiled and saluted, disappearing round the corner.

I closed the door.

This was getting complicated.

I tried to put the police out of my mind while I showered and made myself a cup of coffee. It didn't work. After nervously rushing through breakfast I went for a walk around the fountain, then around the complex, and then throughout the neighbourhood, patrolling cautiously to see if Inspector Longstaff was lurking nearby with his notepad.

He was nowhere to be found.

I breathed a little easier and took a circuitous route back to Stony Creek Estates. I dropped off my chess move outside Henry's door. I could hear his voice inside, gently correcting a technician in German.

Once back in my house, I fell on the pile of mail with a vengeance.

There was a folder for Grace. The return address was the university dorms, so I assumed it was the essay she had mentioned. I set it aside. Noah had received another vet bill for Patton, and Jenny had another letter from her sister.

I set the kettle to boil and walked over to Noah's to drop off the bill.

He was outside the door when I arrived, fiddling with his key in the lock. Patton sat panting at his feet in the most upright position I'd seen him in to date. Drooping in Noah's right hand was a wilting bouquet of flowers. Geraniums.

He greeted me with a snappy, "Mornin' Melville." I handed over the bill and he glanced at it and tossed it to the ground. In a surprisingly spry movement, Patton snatched up the letter and trotted into the house, vanishing down the hallway into one of the rooms with his prize. Noah stood at the door and looked at me expectantly.

"Anything else?" He started to ease the door closed with his foot, his eyes all the while attached to mine in sarcastic curiosity.

"Who gave you the flowers?" I found myself asking.

Noah's face darkened. "No one." He dropped the bouquet onto the hallway floor. Patton's head peeked around the door to his room, but he had no interest in floral arrangement, and he shuffled back out of sight.

Noah nudged the bouquet behind the door and closed it forcefully with a curt, "Mind your business."

Jenny's letter didn't take long to open.

Dear Jenny,

I'm writing from back in Seattle. I'm so glad I was able to get away for a while. Hawaii was wonderful, and I wish you could have seen it with me. I know I said I wouldn't be on you about getting you out and about, but I feel as if I have to, before the end.

[81]

There, I've said it. The doctor says that the three months was an overlong estimate, and I don't have as long as he thought I did. It's so hard writing all this down. I wish I could call you and hear your voice. I hope you get this before it's too late. I want to see you again.

It seems like this letter is full of bad news with no good to balance it. My lawyer says that I won't be able to pay my part of your rent anymore, once I'm gone. What little we have left needs to go to Mark and the kids. I'm sorry.

I know you like getting mail from outside, but I'm afraid that it takes too long to deliver back and forth. Please email me, even if you can't call.

Now is not the time for either of us to be alone.

I love you Jenny. More than words can say.

Your sister,

Cathy

PS. I'll send you a postcard.

Cathy included her email address on a Post-It on the back of the letter.

I deliberated for a moment, and then snatched up my laptop. I didn't know Jenny at all, I had no idea if she would call or email her sister. But I knew one thing. This was the opportunity I'd been waiting for. Jenny needed rent money. And I had 50,000 dollars.

I quickly typed up an email to Cathy.

Dear Cathy,

You don't know me, but I am a friend of your sister's. I heard about your illness, and I am very sorry. I hope that I can help give you peace of mind. I have recently come into some money, and would like to offer to continue to pay your sister's rent so that she doesn't have to move. I hope that this is ok with you, and if you like we don't have to tell Jenny where the money is coming from. Feel better soon.

Jordan Melville

I read over the email. Ok, so *friend of your sister's* was stretching it, maybe. The rest was fine. On second thought, I deleted *feel better soon* and substituted *yours truly*. It seemed less insensitive.

I pressed Send.

I resealed Jenny's envelope and walked across the courtyard to deliver it. I had decided to knock and see if she would open up to me. I figured she might need a friend soon.

Plus, she was pretty. But I wasn't going to let that get the best of me again.

As I neared her house, I could hear Henry's soaring tenor proclaiming *You'll Never Walk Alone* through an open window. I stopped for a minute to listen. This was my favourite track on his CD. The song filled the courtyard and it seemed as though all the world became a captive audience. The leaves no longer blew about in the dry fountain and the birds stopped their warbling in respect for the greater melody.

The final note faded away and the sun resumed its climb in the sky and the wind sighed its appreciation through the trees.

I walked up to Jenny's front door and knocked, gently.

To my surprise the door was opened almost immediately. Jenny stood framed in the doorway. She was older than I expected. Maybe mid-twenties. She looked beautiful. Her face wasn't the same shy mask as the last time I saw her; instead it shone visibly with happiness.

"Jordan? Hello." Her green eyes sparkled for a moment, and then as the outside invaded her home, began to lose their lustre.

I stuttered quickly through my reasoning for being here, not wanting to lose the image of the girl in the hall before me, but with every passing moment her features sank farther back into shadow and her bright smile slipped into obscurity.

"Thank you." Her voice had faded to a whisper again, and she gently took the letter from my hand. Our fingers touched and she started. Henry began a reprise, and Jenny's face braved the sunlight to look at me once more, her eyes suddenly blazing with intensity as if she were trying to read the pages of my heart.

Come on, Melville. Pull yourself together. I tried to blink away the romantic nonsense that was cropping up in my mind.

Jenny smiled softly and blushed, as if she knew my thoughts. My hand dropped from the letter and Henry's voice suddenly cut off. I heard the sound of a phone ringing next door and knew that there was some sort of technical emergency somewhere in the world. Rapid-fire Japanese poured out of 4A's window. The spell was broken.

Jenny turned to retreat back into the safety of her home, but before she closed the door I spoke.

"Hey. Jenny. If you ever need anyone to talk to... I'm just over there," I finished clumsily, pointing somewhere over my shoulder.

Jenny looked at me curiously, probably wondering why she would ever need someone to talk to. But I knew that we had a connection. She must have felt it too.

I turned and walked away from the door. Henry had hung up the phone and was gliding into the first few notes of *Ave Maria*.

"Jordan?" I turned. Jenny was standing outside her front door, still clinging to it with her left hand.

"Thanks." She flowed back inside and the door closed between us.

Even though I knew what was in the letter Jenny was about to read, it was all I could do to keep from skipping back to my house.

I stood in the elevator on my way up to Grace's room. I had promised her I would visit, and I was determined to do so. In my hands was Henry's CD and the essay for Grace to proofread. I had bypassed the front desk, but I stopped at the nurse's station on Grace's floor to make sure it was okay to visit her. The nurse on duty was bobbing her head to an unheard melody and smiled from ear to ear when she heard who I had come to see.

"Visit Grace? Of course you can!" Her orange hair clashed terribly with her pink scrubs, but her smile outshone both. "She's been very popular today!"

I headed down the hall and turned in at Grace's door. Her room was unchanged since I had last been there two days ago. She still lay in her bed, looking wounded and fragile. Her pink hair bow had been replaced by one of deep yellow. It gave the room an autumn feeling.

Grace turned when she heard my voice and her complexion brightened. She dispensed with the pleasantries quickly and motioned me to take a seat next to her bed. Within moments she had torn into the essay and was neck-deep in split infinitives and comma splices.

I sat for a few minutes and listened to her mutter as she savagely crossed out incorrect punctuation and circled misspelled words. More than once I heard her grunt in disbelief at the writer's inability to write. The sound was often followed by the slow scrawl of a large red question mark next to the debatable paragraph.

After Grace had lost herself in a few pages, I made my way out to the nurse's station again. I asked the nurse for a CD player, and she bustled under a cabinet for a moment while humming ...*Baby One More Time* and then triumphantly placed a small stereo on the counter. I thanked her and headed back to the room.

Grace was still busy with the essay. She made quick work of it, tossing the sheets down towards her feet as she finished critiquing them. I put the CD in the player and started to gather up the disorderly pages.

"That's Henry, isn't it." Grace's small head popped up out of her papers. "I miss hearing his voice from across the courtyard. Did you know, dear, I always liked it best when he sang in some other language. It was as if I could make up my own meanings for the songs. I remember once, he sang the same song three times in a row, practicing, I suppose, and each time I thought the song was about something totally different. The first time it was sad, and the next deliriously happy, and the third time very angry indeed. I'm not sure if it was the way he sang it or the way I heard it that changed."

"Yup," I understated. "He sings pretty good."

"Well."

"Sorry?"

"He sings pretty well. Not pretty good. Sorry dear, but you *have* caught an old school-teacher in a correcting mood. Bad grammar is a pet peeve of mine." Grace's eyes sparkled.

"You know, Noah said that to me when I first moved in." I saw Grace's eyes flash again.

[85]

"That old goat wouldn't know a pronoun if *it* bit *him* on the nose." She looked toward the window. The violets there had been watered recently; a small pool was gathered beneath the pot, caught in the saucer. *Music of the Night* played in the background.

"He came to visit me this morning, you know, dear."

"Oh yes, the nurse told me you were popular today."

"Did she? Popular? Well." Grace primped her flattened hair with a starlet's fashionability. "Rebekah's a dear girl. Very efficient." She lay back on her bed and tossed away the final pages of the essay. She continued, "Such a silly old man. He brought me flowers, you know. Geraniums. I do hate geraniums, but it was a sweet thought. Then he saw the violets on the windowsill. Such a jealous, silly old man. I must say, I did play it up. Told him I had an admirer. He went off in a huff, but I forgive him. He always has looked out for me. And my family." She suddenly looked at me with great seriousness in her face. "I do hope he hasn't mistreated those poor geraniums. It's not their fault, you know dear, that I have a young devotee."

I blushed and scrambled to pick up the last remaining sheets. Grace laughed as she watched me, her wispy voice breaking out into a healthy guffaw. "Oh Jordan, you do bring me great joy in my old age. Why, I feel as though I've known you for a lifetime, although that's quite impossible, isn't it? I've never been one to believe in reincarnation, have you? Perhaps you do. I feel that it is a belief for the young. Quite frankly, once you've lived to be my age, the idea of living life all over again is terribly exhausting."

She yawned as she spoke and I took my cue to go.

"Tell young Henry that I love his CD. And the doctors say I might be able to come home soon, so warn Noah to keep that miserable dog away from my hedgehogs."

I didn't go straight home. I knew that I had more research to do, so like any good student I went to the public library. There were two names on my to-do list.

Noah Foster.

Ian Fox.

Of all my neighbours, these were the two whose history I was most curious about.

Fox first. My view of him was the most unclear.

I'd already tried Google, but the library hadn't placed all its archives online yet, so I headed straight to the newspaper archive room. Fox's children were named Jeffery and Alison. An archive search brought up little information. Just a single obituary.

Jeffery Ian Fox
Born January 12, 1985 – Deceased April 12, 1994
&
Alison Mary Fox
Born September 7, 1988 – Deceased April 12, 1994

Both of Ian's children were dead.

There followed a careful selection of biographical information intended to fool the reader into believing that the children had lived long and happy lives, but the grief was printed raw into the ink, and it was clear to all that the children had been taken before their time.

One sentence closed the notice.

They are survived by their father, Ian Fox,
and by their mother, Colleen Fox.

Both Jeffery and Alison had died on the same day. The parents had survived. I remembered from the picture that Fox's wife had been pregnant, but no mention was made of the unborn child.

I made what I could of the facts. They'd died on the same day, a year or so after the picture in Fox's hallway was taken, if the date on his shirt was correct. The wife was still alive, but obviously no longer with Fox. That didn't surprise me. Losing two children would be hard on a marriage.

My questions became more focused. What happened on April 12, 1994? And where is Colleen Fox now?

Another search supplied the answers. Another article, dated Wednesday, April 13, 1994.

Tragic Accident Destroys Local Family
Two Children Dead, Parents in Hospital

Tragedy struck last night in the form of a fatal collision which occurred at a major intersection in Oak Bay. A local father was driving his family home from a school play at around 8:30 PM. Witnesses say that the family vehicle, a red minivan, had stopped at the intersection of Oak Bay Ave. and Foul Bay Rd. when the driver of the minivan began to shout and shake violently. He then accelerated the vehicle into oncoming traffic, where it was hit by a large pickup that was unable to stop. The driver of the truck was unharmed, but two children died at the scene, and the driver of the minivan and a female passenger were taken to hospital. Some witnesses report that the woman was in the late stages of pregnancy. Police and rescue workers have not released the names of the victims, and are not willing to comment at this time on the cause of the collision.

The story was continued the following week on Monday the 17th. This time it was above the fold. The headline said it all.

Local Couple Released from Hospital
New Father Being Held for Questioning
in Children's Deaths

A Google search at a nearby terminal provided a final article. A local family values watchdog group posted the conclusion of a court case which proclaimed that:

Controversial Ruling
Frees Accused Father

Ian Fox, father of collision victims Jeffery and Alison Fox was found innocent today on the charge of negligent vehicular homicide. In a ruling that is already proving to be unpopular, Judge Parnell Wilson supported the Defendant's claim of mental disorder, finding that Fox was not in control of his actions on the night of his children's deaths. The ruling was based on the testimony of Fox's therapist, Dr. Vincent Collingwood, who reported that Fox had long been subject to a variety of mental disorders, and had been taking medication that had proven to be generally effective. Fox testified that he had taken his medication on the evening of the collision, and had never before had such a reaction. His lawyer released a statement saying that "Mr. Fox is pleased with the judge's verdict, but is painfully aware that the clearing of his name will not bring back his children. He asks that you respect his privacy in this difficult time." The ex-wife of the defendant, Colleen Tremont, was present at the ruling, along with her third child by Ian Fox, Emily Tremont. She declined to comment on the verdict.

The picture was taking shape. I leaned back in my chair in the archives. Fox had once been a pretty normal guy. With issues, sure, but who didn't have issues?

Then came the night of the school play. An unknown side-effect, an uncontrollable catastrophe, and a family destroyed.

[89]

My blurry image of the Fox I knew suddenly came into sharp focus. A man, struggling with a terrible disorder, haunted by the deaths of his children at his own hands. His wife leaves him, and who would blame her, and takes his third child with her. And worst of all, he is forced to publicly declare his insanity under oath. It was a self-fulfilling prophecy.

I shuddered. It was no wonder that Fox had retreated from the world, rejected the available medication, and feared organized society. They were the very things that had stolen his life away from him, forced him to jump into the black hole he was now tumbling through, day after day after day.

I recalled what he'd said about the family photo on his wall.

"It was an accident. Forget it."

I bet he wished he could. For all that he had lost himself, it was clear from his reaction in the living room last week that he was unable to rid himself of those memories.

I leaned forward and pecked away at my keyboard. I had come too far to turn back now. A quick search revealed that Colleen Tremont had passed away two years ago. Her daughter, however, was still alive and well. I found Emily Tremont's information on Facebook and copied down her email address. She was just a baby when this all happened, she would be 17 now.

If Ian had disappeared from the world when she was born, then she might not even know that he was still alive. I doubt Ian knew where *she* was.

I started to type my second awkward and intrusive email of the day.

Dear Emily,

You don't know me but I'm a friend of your father's. I'm not sure how much you know about your family's history, but I know that you are alone now. So is he. I think it would be good for him to see you. Please consider meeting with him. I know I have no right to ask this, or even to be involved in your family business, but your father needs some support and I don't think anyone else can give it to him.

Please reply.

Jordan Melville

I pressed Send. Once it was gone, irretrievable and conclusive, a wave of relief swept over me. But I wasn't finished at the library yet. Emotional undertow pulled me back into my research. I was finally going to fulfill my promise.

Help Noah.

The Military Archives were on the other side of the room. I wandered through the stacks, gazing up at the shelves as they climbed over each other on their way to the ceiling. The high shelving units seemed to lean in as they rose, imposing their memories on the information-hungry historian.

So much history. I felt oppressed by the amount of death recorded in the books that lined the passageways like so many hieroglyphics memorializing a tomb.

I found the section I wanted down the fifth aisle. The Korean War. I pulled down a volume marked *Record of Canadian Officers Serving in Korea; 1950-1953.* An index at the back served my purposes and I soon found the listing I was looking for.

> *Lieutenant Colonel Noah Matthew Foster.*
> - *Commander, Delta Company, 2nd Battalion, Princess Patricia's Canadian Light Infantry.*
> - *As a Major, was awarded the Military Cross for Bravery and Meritorious Conduct during the Battle of Kapyong, 1951.*
> - *Promoted to Lieutenant Colonel, July 29, 1958.*
> - *Honourably discharged, October 12, 1964.*

There followed Noah's entire war record, which was impressive. He had been in command of an infantry company that had been charged with the defence of Hill 677 during the Battle of Kapyong. His company had been surrounded by Chinese troops in the night, and cut off from aid, Noah had had to make a very difficult decision.

He'd given the order for Canadian artillery units to bombard his own position. His men had dug in, and most had remained unharmed. The Chinese were unable to advance, and in the morning the 2nd Battalion had secured Hill 677. Noah was proclaimed a hero.

He had returned to Canada in the fall of 1951 and worked as a training officer in Calgary until his retirement in 1964.

When apparently he had decided to move to BC to buy and manage a housing complex.

I closed the book and returned it to the shelf. No wonder Noah didn't want to remember the war. He'd been forced to bomb his own men. And it seemed the Veterans Association was using this Memorial Unveiling as an opportunity to trot him out as a war hero. Noah's surliness suddenly made sense.

His was trying to forget the ghosts of his past.

And the world was celebrating them.

I returned to perusing the shelves. There was one more theory I had to test. I eventually found the thick volume I was looking for laying open on a nearby desk.

Record of Canadian Wounded and Casualties; Korea, 1950-1953. I searched the table of contents for the Battle of Kapyong. Page 176. I flipped hurriedly through the pages. Once there, I scanned down the list, running my finger over the past, looking for a name I knew I would find.

There it was.

Deceased. April 24, 1951. Master Corporal William Ryan Parker. D Company, 2nd Battalion, PPCLI.

William Parker.

Grace's brother Bill.

Tuesday, August 26

My alarm went off at 7:29. I checked to make sure it was still unplugged. It was. The damn thing ran on batteries. I dropped the power cord to the floor and shrugged in defeat. At least it was getting closer.

I wandered outside and grabbed the pile of mail. Being seen in just my boxers had once been unnerving, now it was just another part of my daily routine. I imagined that my neighbours had lists on their walls, hidden under ugly paintings, which chronicled my choice of undergarment as the weeks went by.

Bills and other boring items today. A dental check-up reminder on a postcard for Henry, a BCHydro bill for Noah, and a bank statement for L&S. I did a tour of the complex and dropped them all off at the correct doors. Bills and statements I had no interest in.

The final envelope in the pile hadn't been mailed. Henry had dropped off his next chess move sometime in the night, no doubt in between calls from Latvia and the DRC.

I tore it open as I re-entered my house. It was one sentence long.

You don't want to do that.

I stood over the chess set on my kitchen table and contemplated my last move. It looked fine to me, but I bowed to the master, and graciously took it back. Fine. I'd follow in the footsteps of our Argentinean friend.

Knight to e3.

I scampered back to Henry's door and laid my new move under the mat. I could hear his voice inside. He was labouring to convince some foreign tech to try a different way of fixing the problem. His language vacillated between Spanish and English, and as I turned back to my house I heard him swear in German.

I've never liked the harshness of the German language for communicating, but it is tops for swearing.

I sat at the table, sipping my cup of coffee. My to-do list for the day was short, due to the lack of mail. I had to go to the bank to deposit my cheques. I couldn't leave them around here, not with the police snooping around, and if I wanted to use the money to pay Jenny's rent, I needed it in the bank.

I also had to mail the essay back to the university dorms.

And then, for the third time, I wanted to visit Grace. I needed to ask her about Bill. And Noah.

My laptop chimed. I had mail.

The message was short.

Dear Jordan,

Thank you for your interest in the welfare of the sister of my client. I regret to inform you that Cathy passed away two days ago. Her husband is grateful for your concern, but cannot respond to your enquiry personally as he is understandably mourning the loss of his wife and comforting his children. It is his feeling that if you would like to assist Jennifer in the payments of her tenancy agreement, that is between you and her.

Best wishes,

Joshua Lonsdale
Fellaway, Lonsdale, & Stritch, Solicitors

It was too late for Jenny to call her sister now.

Footsteps sounded in the courtyard. The murmuring *thwick-thwick* of men's dress shoes. I rushed to the front window. A man in a suit was standing at Jenny's door, knocking sharply. After a moment, the door opened a crack. I couldn't hear what was said, but the apologetic droop of the man's shoulders and the sudden slamming of the door spoke volumes. The man wedged a business card into the doorframe and left.

I didn't know what to do. Did I have a responsibility to Jenny because I knew about her sister? Or should I just pretend I knew nothing and let her suffer alone? She'd probably prefer to be alone.

I went to take a shower.

I was pulled from the shower by a frantic pounding on my door. I rushed down the length of my house, dripping wet, wrapped in a towel. The water still ran behind me, and steam flooded the hallway.

I opened the door, interrupting the frenzied tattoo.

It was Jenny.

Her eyes were red and puffy. They darted around behind me, exploring my hallway.

"Jordan. I need to come in."

I stepped aside, very aware that I was clad only in a towel, and Jenny rushed past me into the house. She hurried halfway down the hallway, glanced into my bedroom and turned left, heading into the kitchen. I followed her slowly and found her sitting on the couch, her hands clasping her knees with nervous energy. I was stunned to see her outside of her own house, and told her so.

"I know. I know. But your house is so similar to mine, only dirtier, so it's not too bad..." Her voice shook as she spoke, and I knew that it had taken her a huge effort to come here. But then, she'd had a huge shock.

"You said if I ever needed a friend..." Her voice trailed off and then in a whisper she said, "I didn't know where else to go."

I sat down on the chair and carefully arranged the towel. "Hey, anything you need."

Jenny's lips tried to curve into a smile but were interrupted by a wave of emotion. She sat on my couch and cried, and I sat on my chair and kept my hands on my legs, unsure of the proper course of action. A comforting hand would normally be ok in this situation, but not with an agoraphobe, and not when the comforter is naked.

I went for the soothing therapist approach. "Just let it all out."

She did.

I got up and got her some toilet paper from the bathroom, taking the opportunity to throw on some clothes on the way back to the living room. Jenny had stopped sobbing, but was still sitting on the couch, her head facing down and her knees and her hands shaking.

I handed her the toilet roll.

"You put some pants on. Thanks," she said as she accepted the tissue.

I sat down again. "You wanna talk about it?"

She sniffled. "I just found out that— that my sister..." Her voice disappeared into a short reprise of sobs. She collected herself. "She just passed away. Cancer." Jenny clutched the tissue in her hand, clenching her fist as if she were holding on to her last memories of Cathy.

"I'm sorry." And I was.

"I was going to go see her this weekend. At least I tell myself that. I had the route all planned out. I don't normally go outside you know."

I said I knew, Noah had told me.

"I only just found out it was really bad. She'd just been away. A vacation. She said she was feeling really good." Jenny started to gasp the short quick breaths of hyperventilation. I told her to try to relax and got her a glass of water.

She brushed her eyes with the toilet paper. "I shouldn't even be sad for her. She'd been ready to go for ages. But I'm not ready. I always thought there would be more time. That's what makes this so bad. She was ready. I'm just selfish."

I shook my head and made comforting noises.

"No, you don't know the worst part. She paid most of my rent. Because of my... condition, I can't ever hold down a job, unless I work from home. Right now I just format newsletters for a few community groups. It barely pays anything!" A tear leaked out of her left eye and trailed down her face. "So now I have to move before September starts! I don't even know what upsets me more. I'm such a terrible sister!" She broke down completely.

I sat in my chair, frozen. These levels of emotions, conflicting yet building on one another, were out of my league.

I only had one thing to offer.

"Jenny." She looked up at me through her tears as if surprised at my presence. Her eyes flared and her hand flew to her throat suddenly. She visibly tensed and then shook her head, her eyes darting around the room, taking in the familiar shapes and dimensions of the room. She relaxed again.

"Jenny," I repeated. "If you would let me, I can help cover your rent for the next little while. Until we can figure something out."

Her mouth opened and released its shape with a tiny, "oh..." She stared at me for a few moments and then shook her head again. "No. I can't let you. I can't take your money."

I tried to interrupt but she ran over my words with a force I'd never seen from her.

"No. It's very sweet of you, but I can't accept. Cathy was right. It's time for me to grow up and face the world. I can't be alone forever." Her voice was strong and firm, excepting a small quaver as she spoke the last word.

She stood and walked around the corner to the door, brushing her hand along the wall as she went, keeping contact with the familiar structure. She opened the door and visibly steeled herself for the long walk back to her unit. Which wouldn't be her unit for much longer.

Jenny looked over her shoulder at me, her eyes were still red and puffy, but they now held a determination. "Thanks Jordan. I know we don't know each other very well, but I appreciate your friendship all the same." She turned back to the world, squared her shoulders and quick-marched across the courtyard, quickly disappearing into 3A.

Well, that hadn't gone at all as I'd planned. I'd just spent the morning naked with the girl-next-door, and all I was left with was a pile of snotty toilet paper and the F-word.

Friendship.

The steam from the bathroom started to fog up the living room window, obscuring my view.

I decided it was a metaphor for my life and, sighing, went to finish my shower. I still had errands to run.

I emerged from the bank, feeling like a million bucks. Or at least like 50,000 bucks. Financial security was a beautiful thing. And the police were none the wiser. I turned the corner and ran headlong into an oncoming pedestrian.

It was Inspector Longstaff.

"Ah, good morning Jordan. Fancy meeting you here. Just been to the bank, eh? Hope your balance is swinging in your favour. Say, have you got any *inside information* for me?" He winked. "Don't worry about it. I'm sure we'll bump into one another again. Catch you later!" He threw that last over his shoulder and sauntered into the bank.

I high-tailed it out of there.

A brisk walk took me on a zigzag route to the bus stop. I passed a mailbox on the way and threw the essay in. That student was going to have a lot of editing to do. The amount of red ink Grace had added to the papers seemed to double the weight of the package.

The bus pulled up and took me on a whiplash journey that soon had me disembarking at the hospital entrance.

I greeted Rebekah as I passed the nurse's station. She was humming *All the Single Ladies* by Beyoncé and she waved her hand at me as I passed by, flipping it from back to palm and back again. *Uh-oh-oh, oh-oh-oh...*

Grace was looking much better today. She was lying in her bed when I entered and her face glowed with renewed vigour as she greeted me. She used a small remote to turn down Henry's CD.

"Jordan! Two days in a row! I am a lucky girl. What brings you by so suddenly, dear? You look as though you have something on your mind, no, don't deny it; I have a sixth sense about these things. Unburden yourself to an old woman. I'm a wonderful listener you know."

Well, I wasn't going to tell her about Fox's family history, or about the Gordon sisters' secret hobby, or about Sasha's kidney. But as I sat down I found myself telling her all about Jenny. How I felt about her, the letters from her sister, the fact that she wouldn't accept my help and would have to move out of the complex.

Grace listened patiently and didn't interrupt once. When I was finished she clicked her tongue and smiled. "Well, I'm glad you took my advice to heart. Anyone can read into people's lives Jordan; it takes a special kind of person to want to do something good about it. Now, I didn't expect you to take Jenny to heart too, but I can't say I'm shocked. She is such a lovely girl. She needs someone to take care of her."

Her face brightened. "Say, that's an idea. Someone to take care of her. Jordan, be a dear and get me some paper and a pen from Rebekah, won't you?"

Rebekah was facing away from the counter, busily bringing sexy back with Justin Timberlake, and I had to clear my throat awkwardly to catch her attention. She supplied me with the items and I returned to Grace's room.

She was now sitting up and had pulled her table in front of her. Taking the pen and paper, she started to write, and explained to me as she went.

"Someone to take care of her. That's what made me think of it, dear. A real brainwave, as you kids say. Just this morning I heard the doctor say the same to thing to one of the other nurses. Of course, he was talking about me. I gave him a piece of my mind after that, I assure you, but then you arrived and this little idea pops into my head. You say Jenny needs a place to stay, and here I am thinking that we both need someone to take care of us. Why, it couldn't be more perfect. And of course, she can't say no. After all, I'm an old woman and I need the help. She'll be doing me the favour. Oh, I must write that in... *You'll be doing me a favour.* There. Jordan, be a dear and deliver this for me will you? What a wonderful thing it is to help people. And to think, it all came about because of me. Thank you, dear."

Grace handed me the folded up paper and took a few deep breaths. "This really will be for the best. Now that poor girl doesn't have to uproot herself. Goodness knows how hard that is for anyone, let alone someone in her condition. And now Noah can rent out her unit in time for the school semester to start, so that old blowhard can't complain about it. Perfect." She chuckled softly in a very self-congratulatory manner.

I took the opening she presented.

"Grace? About Noah. I did some research." Her eyes sharpened. "I know that your brother was under Noah's command in the war."

"Yes, our families were old friends. Bill and Noah went through basic training together. Of course, Bill was never as bright as Noah was, so he stayed behind while Noah advanced through the officers training. But they remained fast friends." Grace's face was softened with the shadows of the past. I persisted.

[99]

"But then, if you were all such close friends, why are you two always fighting now?" Her gaze flicked towards me. I sputtered an addendum, "If you don't mind me asking."

Grace smiled a little and turned her head towards the window. "It's not the asking I mind, Jordan. It's the telling."

She fell silent, and I stood to leave. As I reached the door her voice caught me.

"They shipped out together. It was 1950. By that time Noah was already a Major, but my Bill was still a Master Corporal. They shipped out to Pusan, where Noah proceeded to get Bill into all sorts of trouble, usually with girls. Bill was always so handsome."

I turned back towards the bed. Grace was still staring out the window, and a single tear ran down her cheek.

"There was a big battle. I don't remember the name, but it was the red Chinese against forces from the American, Australian, and Canadian armies."

"Kapyong," I murmured.

"Kapyong, that was it. They had to hold a hill. I assume it was a very important hill, but I never really understood why. Noah's company had been forced to retreat and the Chinese had surrounded him. He lost some men, but not many. As the night went on, the shelling got worse and worse. The Chinese had closed in and Noah had to call in support from some other Canadian troops. They began to fire on his position. He had only a few moments to warn his men to find cover, and then the shells began to drop. Most of the men survived. The Chinese retreated and Noah's battalion retook the hill. It was in all the papers. Everyone in town was talking about it. Noah was a hero, and I was a hero by association. But Bill was the greatest hero of us all. After the hill had been reclaimed, Noah found Bill's body. He hadn't survived the shelling, but whether it was the Canadian or Chinese artillery that got him, no one ever knew. Noah always assumed the worst. When he came back, we attended Bill's service together. That night he broke off our engagement."

I sat down in the chair, unwilling to interrupt, but Grace turned to look at me. Her face was now flooded with tears. They traced the lines of her wrinkles down her face, marking her connection to the past with shining streaks.

"Oh yes. We were very much in love. We still are, as far as I know. But Noah could never forgive himself for what he'd had to do. For what he *may* have taken away from me. I still wanted him of course, but he forbade it. He stayed on the base for years before he finally moved here and bought Stony Creek." A stubborn smile cracked through the veil of memories. "He wasn't going to get away from me that easily. I moved in."

I couldn't help laughing. Grace's feisty demeanour didn't allow for pity, and her eyes sparkled in appreciation.

"And I've been the perfect tenant. Never given him cause for complaint, or eviction. The old blowhard was stuck with me for better or for worse, only without any of the benefits." She laughed the last few tears away. "Stubborn old fool."

I stood again. Grace reached out and took my hand.

"You know dear, you're not a bad listener yourself."

I leaned in and kissed her on the forehead. She closed her eyes and smiled.

I knocked on Jenny's door. She looked through the hazy window and saw me. The door opened and she smiled nervously.

"Well, we seem to be seeing a lot of each other," I said. She laughed politely. I could hear Henry's voice softly echoing from inside the house. That CD was everywhere.

"I have a note for you. It's from Grace." I held the paper out to her. She took it and looked at it for a minute, hesitating, and then looked up at me decidedly.

"Please come in."

She stood aside to let me pass into the house. I idly wondered how many others had been allowed onto this hallowed ground. I turned into the living room. It was immaculate. Simple and plain furniture hugged the walls. Family pictures dotted the empty space above them, in single frames and large collages. My eye travelled around the room, taking in Jenny's pictorial history. There she was as a child, often partnered with a much older girl in a variety of photo ops. Buried in the sand at the beach. Hugging a tree with a red tent in the background. Clustered around a table with other children, waiting for the guest of honour to blow out the candles. Bouncing on her parents' bed, pulling at the blankets and carrying trays of soggy cereal and burnt toast.

Farther down the wall Jenny's life became more sedate. Pictures with friends came few and far between. In one Jenny stood at her graduation in cap and gown. In another, she sat at her desk, feverishly scribbling the last few lines of an essay due the next day while Cathy read on the couch behind her with a baby. There was a picture of a pregnant Cathy sunning herself on the lawn. The photo was framed by the window through which Jenny had taken it.

At the end of the wall was one final picture. Cathy, beaming from her hospital bed, surrounded by friends and family. She was holding a newborn baby in her arms. Jenny wasn't in that picture. I guessed that she wasn't the photographer either.

I turned to find her standing in the doorway to the living room, nervously twisting her hands at this invited intrusion into her privacy.

"It's nice." I moved to a chair, and shifted a pile of mail-order catalogues out of the way. "You should read Grace's note."

She nodded, gratefully for the cue, and sank into the couch beneath the window. I watched her face as she read each line, and saw her eyes widen with the knowledge that she could stay at Stony Creek.

She looked up to me, her face seeking confirmation of the truth.

"Grace said she needs someone who can always be around, just in case," I said, inventing rapidly. "She hoped you might help her out, if you didn't mind moving across the way. You'd have your own room, and—"

I was interrupted by the impact of Jenny's arms pulling me into a crushing hug. I felt her chest against mine, and her warmth spread throughout my body. As quickly as she came, she backed away, her eyes wide with the shock of what she had just done.

"Oh. Oh, I'm so sorry. I'm so sorry, Jordan." She ran over my attempts to placate her. "I just... with all that's happened... for Grace to be so kind... for you to be so kind..."

She looked down and smoothed her hair behind her ear. "I couldn't leave. Everything I have left is here." She looked up at me. "Everyone I have left is here." She turned suddenly and rushed down the hall into the furthest bedroom. The door slammed behind her, and I could hear her crying.

I hesitated in the front hallway. The door behind me seemed the most sensitive choice. I opened it quietly and stopped when I heard Jenny's voice from down the hall.

"Come back tomorrow and help me pack?"

I nodded, closed the door gently behind me and floated back to my house.

Wednesday, August 27

The morning couldn't come soon enough. I didn't wait to see what time my alarm would go off; I was up and showered, and sitting in my kitchen with my coffee by 5:00 AM.

There was only one piece of mail on my chair this morning.

It was a third letter from CSIS to Fox.

Dear Mr. Fox,

It is with the gravest concern that I write this letter. I am afraid I must indeed confirm your suspicions that the Salvation Army Seniors Show Choir is a cover for the Mossad's activities in Canada. I would warn you to keep your distance, or if you must hear them perform, plug your ears during the entire third chorus of "Climb Every Mountain."

Due to your inventive understanding of the intelligence community, you will no doubt be pleased to hear that I have taken the liberty of forwarding your warnings to various members of my entire department. We all receive great joy from your correspondence, and hope it maintains its cutting-edge originality for a long time to come. As always,

Yours,

John Haffner
Assistant Director (Intelligence)
CSIS

I set the letter down with a shaking hand. Last week I would have joined in with the laughter. But no longer. I grabbed my laptop and found the contact information for online CSIS inquiries. I wrote in the same pseudo-serious mocking tone that Haffner loved so much.

Dear Mr. Haffner

*It is with the gravest concern that **I** write this letter. I have been privy to your communications with Mr. Ian Fox, and find your remarks deplorable. Mr. Fox is a human being, who has his own issues to deal with and is not helped by your cavalier attitude.*

You are encouraging a man in unhealthy delusions. I am sure this must be some sort of violation of human rights. Perhaps your "Grey Area" could let you in on the legalities.

I sincerely hope that your response to Mr. Fox's condition is not indicative of the state of Canadian "intelligence" today.

*For Mr. Fox's sake, and for the sake of his friends and family, I hope to **not** hear from you soon. As always,*

Yours,

Jordan Melville

I had to use the online thesaurus a few times, but I think I got my point across. I clicked send with a malicious relish and noticed that a new message had popped up in my inbox as I had typed. It was from Emily Tremont. Speak of the devil.

Hey Jordan, this is kind of weird, some random guy writing me about my dad. But I guess I'm ok with weird, cause I'm writing back, so... whatever. Look, my mom told me all about everything when I was 12. I never wanted to find my dad then, and I don't much want to find him now. Esp. if he's still crazy. It's nice what you're doing n all, but I'm just not into the whole "modern family" thing right now. I'm fine with my life as is. Ok?

Emily

I wasn't really surprised at her response. What 17 year-old girl wants to get involved with an insane family member? But I was still on fire from writing my scalding letter to CSIS, so I thought I'd give it one more shot. For Ian's sake.

Hi Emily,

I know it's crazy for me to keep on you like this, but hear me out. I come from a pretty normal family. House in the suburbs, white picket fence, 2.4 kids, the works. I know this, because I'm the 0.4 kid. I moved out so that I could find the real world, and I found your dad. He's alone, and every day he spends alone is another day he has no one to listen to but the voices in his head. He needs a family, and you're all he has.

I know that sounds super-dramatic, but it's true. One of our neighbours' sisters just died. They weren't able to see each other before it happened and they were both pretty broken up about it. The sister sent a letter to my neighbour two days before she died. She wrote, "Now is not the time for either of us to be alone."

Please think about it. You might need him as much as he needs you.

Jordan

I sent the message. Hopefully Emily would come around. It was all I could do for Ian.

There was a knock at the door. I set down my coffee and headed down the hall.

It was Henry.

"Hey Jordan, Jenny asked me to get you. She said you were going to help her pack?" I nodded. "I figured if she was packing, she could have some of my boxes. You know, the CD boxes?"

"Great idea. Are they still at your place?" He said yes and we headed over to pick them up.

As we walked I casually asked the obvious question. "So, how did you know Jenny was moving?"

Henry let out a small squeak as he tripped over a paving stone. "Oh, uh, I was dropping off a CD for her, and she was in the middle of packing, so... I offered."

I frowned. "Another CD? She already had one when I was there yesterday."

It was Henry's turn to frown as we walked through his door. "She wanted one for... a gift. You were there yesterday too?"

"Oh sure." I grabbed three of the empty flattened boxes that were waiting by the door. "Jenny and I are close."

"Oh." Henry's frown deepened. We circumnavigated his Zen garden and arrived at Jenny's door. I knocked. Her voice echoed from down the hall.

"Come in!"

I opened the door, tossed my boxes in and turned to Henry. He was peering over my shoulder down the hall. I grabbed the fourth box from him, and with as much cheer as I could muster said, "Thanks Henry! I won't keep you," and closed the door.

No hard feelings, Henry. You may be the chess champion, but this game has different rules.

Jenny appeared from a room down the hall. "Hi Jordan. Did I hear Henry?"

"He just dropped off these boxes. He's gone now."

Jenny swooped down on the boxes and carried them into the living room. Her demeanour towards me had changed dramatically. I knew that I was an accepted member of a very small club. In the safety of her own house she could feel free to... well, to feel free.

"Oh, he's so sweet." Jenny admired the boxes.

I feigned gruffness, imitating Noah. "And what am I, chopped liver?"

Jenny giggled. "You're sweet too." She hurried into the kitchen for a tape gun. If I hadn't known her sister had just died and she was being forced from her home, I'd never have guessed from her manner. Maybe she was in denial.

I turned into the living room.

Jenny did not need help packing. It was already done.

The walls were empty of photographs; any holes had already been filled with toothpaste in hopes of a returned security deposit. All of the

[107]

furniture was covered with plastic sheeting, awaiting the new tenant. In the centre of the room was a mound of boxes; each one labelled by room. Below each label was a listing of every item in the box. To my left by the door was a massive pile of catalogues which leaned precariously against the wall, waiting impatiently for the chance to fall into one of Henry's boxes. The only other items left unpacked were an assortment of pictures spread out on the kitchen table.

Pictures of Cathy.

From grade school to the present, it seemed like every picture that Jenny had of her sister was evenly distributed over the surface of the table.

Jenny noticed my interest from the kitchen. She came round to the table, tape gun in hand.

"I couldn't bear to put them away. It felt too much like a burial." The confident, fun-loving Jenny had retreated back into her shell. Her bottom lip quivered.

I leapt to the rescue.

"Would you like me to do it?" Jenny nodded and pulled out a well-used tissue from her pocket. She put her brave face back on.

"I'll build the boxes." She rushed over to the living room entrance and knelt, wrapping the large cardboard boxes in a cocoon of packing tape.

I carefully began to sort the pictures into piles by estimated date. Cathy's life passed through my hands and into the box. I felt Jenny come up behind me.

"That one was taken at Thetis Lake. I was 6 and Cathy was 19. Even with our age difference, Cathy never skipped out on family events. She was always there for me." Jenny's voice dropped to a whisper.

I picked up another picture. "What about this one?"

A nervous giggle. "That was Halloween. Cathy dressed up as Dr. Evil, and I was Mini-Me."

"I like you bald." I held the picture up to her face and compared the two. "You should try the look again."

She snatched the picture away from me and grabbed another off the table.

"Ok. Where do you think we took this one?"

I stepped out into the courtyard. Jenny and I had just spent three hours going through her old pictures. It was a cathartic experience. Jenny had laughed and cried, and cried some more, but she seemed to be feeling much better now.

Now to get the keys from Grace and move Jenny in.

I crossed over to the fountain and saw Henry stepping out of Grace's front door. He was holding a set of keys.

"Hi Jordan." He smiled. "I thought I could help out by swinging by the hospital and getting Grace's keys. I've moved everything out of the second bedroom for now; Grace said you and her can figure out how to redecorate the rest of the house when she's back." He said the last part over my shoulder, smiling up at Jenny who had come to her front door to see me off.

Check. I made a note not to underestimate the chess nerd.

"Do you want to go over first, or do you want me to start carrying boxes over?" I wasn't going to be outmanned by geeky Henry, genius or not.

"I think..." She faltered.

Henry and I spoke at the same time. "No rush!"

We looked at each other and grinned.

Stalemate. A truce, for now.

Jenny finished her thought without looking at us. "I think... I'll go over first. But alone." She glanced down at us apologetically.

We both waved her words away. She gingerly crossed the courtyard, stepping carefully and slowly as she stretched herself from her sanctuary. At the halfway point, just as she passed the fountain, her allegiance visibly shifted and started to pull her in the direction of Grace's house. Jenny's and Grace's house.

She practically bolted through the door.

Henry's eyes followed her in. "Interesting girl."

"Very interesting." I was staring at the door too.

There was a moment of silence. Then Henry spoke.

"You're too young for her."

"You're too old for her."

"I saw her first, newbie."

"In your dreams, poindexter."

We looked at each other and laughed. Henry shook my hand and I clapped him on the shoulder. We had a perfect understanding. Jenny had a decision to make, but we'd already made ours.

I followed Henry back to his place for a demonstration on the proper management of an online empire while I made my specialty, Grilled Cheese Sandwich Surprise.

The secret's in the peanut butter.

Thursday, August 28

I awoke in the morning with sore muscles and a roiling stomach-ache. The former was due to the movement of boxes from Jenny's old house to her new house. The latter was due to an overindulgence of peanut butter. My only consolation was that Henry was feeling worse than me on both counts. I'd made sure he carried the boxes of catalogues.

To redeem myself to him, I'd set aside the day for my Henry project. I had already worked on Fox, worked with Jenny, and worked for Louise and Sylvia. Noah and Grace were works in progress, and Sasha was... Sasha.

My idea was simple: One, Henry had an amazing voice. Two, very few people knew about Henry's amazing voice. Three, I was going to put on a CD sale in the courtyard. Flyers all around the neighbourhood, speakers by the fountain playing his music, the whole nine yards.

And I wasn't going to tell Henry.

First things first. I went to Noah to get his permission to use the courtyard on Sunday afternoon. He seemed suspicious at first.

"Why doesn't he sell his own CDs?" Noah narrowed his eyes. "Are you getting some sort of commission for this? Because if you are, I'd damn sure better be getting a cut for letting you use my courtyard to host Woodstock."

I assured him that there would be no free love taking place in his precious courtyard and he grudgingly gave permission.

Next I settled down in front of my laptop. I found a picture of Henry on one of his tech support sites and pasted it into a flyer template. I filled in the day and time; Sunday at noon, and wrote a glowing review of Henry's self-titled album, comparing him to Andrea Bocelli, Josh Groban, and Michael Bublé. I considered adding in Justin Bieber, but I thought that might draw the wrong crowd. I saved the file on a memory stick and headed to the door, planning to go to the local print shop and run off a few dozen flyers.

I opened my door and took a step back. Standing directly outside, peering around the doorframe into my living room window, was the pale, drawn face of Inspector Longstaff.

"Hiya there Jordan. I was in the neighbourhood, so I thought I'd drop by to see if you had any news for me."

I shook my head and sidestepped him, closing my door behind me. "I have to go run some errands."

"No problem. I'm heading into town myself. Want a ride? We could chat on the way."

I calmly informed him that my errand was only a few blocks away and I would rather walk, thank you very much.

"Fine, fine. I'll keep you company. Exercise is good for the brain." He set out alongside me. "So what's this mysterious errand you're running? Anything I'd find..." his voice dropped to a whisper, "interesting?"

I sighed and briefly explained about Henry.

"Say, that's fantastic! Love your neighbour, that's a good kid." We stopped to wait for a light to change in silence. The light went green and Longstaff started talking again.

"So you're big into helping your neighbours, eh? Do anything for them, would you?" He shot a glance at me out of the corner off his eye. I yawned.

We arrived at the copy centre. I hesitated by the door, afraid he would follow me in. Longstaff looked at his watch. "Is that the time? I've got to get back to work. I've got 50,000 things to do today, you know what I mean? You're either workin' hard or hardly workin', am I right Jordan?" He punched my arm and started back down the street the way we came.

I turned to the door and pulled it open. A doorbell sounded and the clerk looked up at me just as the inspector's voice reached my ears from the street.

"Oh, and Jordan, I took the liberty of delivering your complex's mail today. It was just sitting there, and I figured since I'm a public servant... well, you know. You stay out of trouble now." And he disappeared around the corner.

The flyers came out great, except for a black smudge on the printer that gave every picture of Henry a pencil-thin, black moustache. I kinda liked it. I spent the afternoon stapling the papers to telephone poles, sticking them in storefront windows, and taping them to the sides of mailboxes.

I ended by handing out flyers to the Stony Creek residents. Fox snatched his from my hand, took one look at Henry's moustache-like smudge and flew into his house. He emerged moments later with a large, blond handlebar moustache stuck to his lip and calmly began to dust his mirrors as if I wasn't there. I think he believed I couldn't recognise him.

Noah eyed the flyer and said that if he found any extras littering up his courtyard he'd consider it perfectly within his rights to increase my rent.

Sasha didn't answer the door, so I slipped one under the mat, out of Noah's view. Jenny cautiously opened Grace's door, but forgot her fears when I told her my plans. I received another awkward hug for my pains.

Louise and Sylvia looked at me amusedly when I came to their door. I explained my idea, and they both brightened considerably. Louise beamed at me, and even Sylvia consented to adjust her grunt to a higher pitch. Louise took the flyer and as I turned to go, Sylvia grabbed my arm.

"Not so fast. We have another job."

I found myself puttering along in the station wagon, head poking out between the two sisters' shoulders, demanding an explanation.

"This is the worst possible time for another job! That cop has been following me around for days, he's probably somewhere behind us right now!" I swivelled in my seat. There were many cars on the highway behind us, and I didn't see Longstaff in any of them. But he was tricky. "Can't the money wait for a while?"

Louise waved at an irate passing motorist. "The money can never wait Jordan."

Sylvia turned and glared at me. "Oh, that cop won't be a problem. He's already spoken to us. We fed him a nice little fairy story and he bought it hook, line, and sinker. Why he's still watching *you*, I don't know. You're not up to something on the side are you?"

I squirmed a little in my seat. She continued, "If you aren't up to it, Bugsy, we can always drop you off. There's the door." She pointed.

I pictured another $50,000 cheque and sat back in my seat. Sylvia pursed her lips and turned forward again.

"Besides," she said, "that's why now is such a good time for another job. They'll never expect us to try it while we know we're being watched."

"We'll catch them off-guard," Louise murmured as she turned off the highway.

I stewed in the back seat as we pulled into the parking lot. It didn't make any sense to me, but they were the experts.

George was waiting for us at the front desk. "Louise. Sylvia. Jordan." He gave each of us a small nod and presented us with our visitor's tags. We were immediately buzzed into the visitor's room and took up our standard positions; me sitting on the bench along the far wall, Louise and Sylvia seated at the desk and Tom, who had been waiting for us, standing next to the prisoner's door. He greeted the sisters and cleared his throat.

The door from the jail was buzzed open and a guard ushered in what looked like a woolly mammoth clad in an orange jumpsuit. He filled the room and dwarfed the Gordon sisters. His dark curly hair fell down past his shoulders and a beard surrounded his face, hiding from view the lower half of an ugly scar that ran down his left cheek. He looked like Angry Jesus. His arms were massive and covered in tattoos. Snakes, skulls, and naked women scrolled up his forearms and into the prison-issue coveralls. He sat down in his chair with an enormous *whump* and glared out at the sisters. Tom opened his mouth.

"*Three little maids from school are we...*"

The prisoner started. He rotated slowly and observed Tom standing rigidly behind him, clasping a truncheon firmly in his hands and emitting a lively falsetto. He turned back to the sisters and a wide smile spread across his face, revealing a number of dark gaps that would make a hockey player proud. "We don't get much call for *The Mikado* around here."

I blinked. Whatever I had expected him to say, that wasn't it.

"You're the Gordon sisters, right?"

Louise nodded and opened her mouth. She didn't get a chance to start the sales pitch.

"Sir James Douglas Elementary School. The gymnasium storage room. At the very back underneath all the old equipment you'll find an old black punching bag with two strips of duct tape on it, like an 'X'. Ten million dollars."

My jaw dropped. He looked up at me and grinned sheepishly. "The vault was open when I got there."

Sylvia leaned forward and opened her mouth. The mammoth cut her off.

"I know, I know, twenty percent. Discretion is your watchword. I've heard all about you. Are you in?"

The sisters looked at each other and nodded slowly.

"Good. One final thing. It's impossible to get in during the week; even at night, there are always extracurricular activities going on." He glanced up at me again. "I used to work there as the janitor," he explained. "Saturday night is your best bet. The school is always clear by 7:00 PM." He stood up and Tom stopped singing.

"Pleasure doing business with you." And he was gone.

We dropped off our passes with George and walked out to the car in silence. Once we had turned onto the highway I burst.

"Come on! It's so obviously a trap for us!" Louise and Sylvia exchanged glances. "Seriously?" I was in disbelief. "You don't see it? He volunteers the information, tells us exactly where to go and when? They'll be waiting for us!"

Louise murmured from the front seat, "No... no I don't think so."

Sylvia agreed. "He was in a rush because it's such a big amount. And left in such a poor hiding spot."

"Why, at any moment a child could decide to take up boxing, and—"

"Poof! There goes 10 million dollars."

"It is a nice round number."

I goggled. "I can't believe you guys are falling for this!"

Sylvia whipped around in her seat. "Look Jordan, this could be the last big job we ever need to pull. This is our retirement fund we're talking about here. If you don't want in, then get out."

Even Louise looked stern as she looked at me through the rear-view mirror. "It's the chance of a lifetime Jordan. We have to take it."

I fell back into my seat. "But it's a trap..."

Sylvia flung herself forward and grunted.

A million reasons not to do it raced through my head. Most of them ended with the phrase "twenty-five to life." But on the other side of my brain flashing dollar signs demanded my attention. My cut would be $200,000. Gold bars and prison bars battled for supremacy, and in between them was one final choice. But as I looked at the two middle-aged women sitting in front of me, the thoughts of prison and money faded away, and I realized why I was really worried.

Somewhere in the last two weeks; in between the tea parties and the sledgehammers, they had become my friends. And I wasn't willing to let them walk into a trap without me there to protect them.

"I'm in."

I got home and was greeted by three new emails. The first was from an electronics rental company. They would drop off a set of large outdoor speakers on Sunday morning. I made a note to make sure Henry was busy on Sunday for the set-up. I wanted it to be a complete surprise.

The second message was from Emily. It read:

Hey Jordan,

My aunt says I'm making a huge mistake. But I've decided. We're going to come by on Saturday at 12ish. Can you send me the address? (And make sure my dad isn't crazy that day?)

Emily

I pumped my fists in the air and did a hula dance. Progress!
The third message cooled me down considerably.

Hiya Jordan,

Just thought I'd drop you a line to say hi. I happened to be out at the prison this evening on business, and imagine my surprise when I saw you driving out of the parking lot! And in such a distinctive car. You really do get around, you seem to be everywhere I go.

I'm glad we can have these little moments. It's good to always remember who your friends are, don't you agree?

See you soon,

Inspector Paul Longstaff
VicPD

I didn't sleep very well that night.

Friday, August 29

The next morning my alarm didn't go off. I woke up at 1:37 PM and I knew the batteries weren't dead because the time was still showing. I grabbed the clock and stared at it, right into its digital display. This time I wouldn't blink first.

"All right, chump. This one is for all the marbles."

43 seconds later, it caved and I set it down in triumph.

I showered and dressed and headed into the kitchen. My first order of business was to send Emily the address for Stony Creek Estates. My usual morning routine had been disrupted again, I assumed by Longstaff, since the day's mail had already been delivered to the appropriate doors before I woke up.

I was starting to get the impression that Inspector Longstaff had a little too much time on his hands.

As I was sipping my coffee there was a knock at my door. Henry had brought over his next move. I waved at the chess board on my kitchen table.

"Go ahead."

He refused, saying that the whole point of playing chess by mail was that I read the move and I moved the piece.

I set my coffee down and tore into the envelope. Inside was a note with Henry's move and a $20 bill. I held the bill up questioningly.

Henry shrugged. "It's Friday. I need you to help me bring the second shipment of CDs home."

I agreed instantly. I'd forgotten that the second shipment was due to arrive today. Perfect timing.

We set off at once, strolling to the post office, complaining about the weather, admiring the scenery, and by and large talking about anything except Jenny. We had come to a mutual understanding that she was off-limits, conversationally at least.

I soon found myself talking about Fox. Henry was interested in his neighbour; although they'd lived in close proximity for seven years, Henry had never once spoken to him.

We arrived at the post office, and as we waited for the clerk to truck out the boxes from the back I gave Henry a short history of Ian's life and revealed that I had convinced Emily to come visit tomorrow.

Henry was delighted. He grinned as he signed for the packages.

"I think that's wonderful! What a great thing to do for a neighbour! Is there anything I can do to help?" he offered generously as he once again left three of the four boxes for me to carry.

I struggled to catch up as he exited the store without a moment's hesitation. Once we were again walking shoulder-to-shoulder I told him I was planning on visiting Ian this afternoon to prepare him for his daughter's visit.

"You're free to join me if you like; I might be able to use the help... although you'll have to be aware of Ian's... temperaments."

Henry winked. "Got it covered. My mom is manic-depressive. I'm used to dealing with people with... issues. No problem."

I was shocked at the casualness that he spoke with.

He noticed. "Look, it's no big deal. Lots of people are bipolar; it's just something a family has to learn to live with. Like diabetes. My mom usually took her medication, but when she was feeling good, sometimes she'd stop and— well, let's just say my dad wasn't the type of guy to deal with things head on. He'd lock himself away in his office, and I'd be left to make sure everything was ok."

We turned the corner and passed through the gate into our complex. Ian's mirrors greeted us, our fractured images cutting jaggedly across his yard. I volunteered to store the CDs in my unit, since I had an empty room. Henry agreed and we shoved the boxes into a corner, easily accessible for Sunday's big music sale.

I told Henry to meet me at Ian's in five minutes, and he went back home.

I walked into my bathroom with a bag and picked up a few items I thought we could use. Then I was out the door. I passed the mirrors and knocked on the door just as Henry came up behind me, another bag hanging over his shoulder.

A shadow moved in the hallway.

Here goes nothing.

Fox unbolted his series of locks and opened the door with a quick jerk. He stared blankly at us in silence.

I spoke, "Hi Ian, you remember me? I'm the guy—"

"You're the mail-boy. And you're the Bill Gates wannabe from three doors down. Whaddaya want?" He seemed remarkably lucid today. And sarcastic.

"I need to talk to you. I have something important to tell you." Ian didn't say anything. I pressed my case. "Can we please come in?"

Ian remained silent but shuffled aside, allowing us to pass into the house.

The hallway hadn't changed. Newspaper articles still papered the walls, but in the light of day they had lost their sinister tone and seemed instead quaintly eccentric.

We turned into the living room. The couch cushions still lay flung about, but I noticed that the cups of sugar were gone. Ian whirled around the room, throwing the cushions back into their places and slid into his seat, breathing heavily, with a look of innocence that seemed to hope we hadn't noticed his tidying.

We seated ourselves.

I figured it was best just to jump right in. "Ian, I know about your family." His expression didn't change. "I know about Jeffery and Alison, and I know that Colleen left." Ian's face quickly darkened at his ex-wife's name. I was suddenly extra-glad of Henry's presence.

I forged ahead. "You remember that Colleen was pregnant?"

His face cleared just as quickly. "Yes. Baby Emily."

And just like that, we'd come to the point. "Well... I found her. I found Emily. And she wants to meet you." I sat back and waited for his response.

It was slow in coming. "Emily." Fox muttered to himself. Henry shifted his weight beside me. "Colleen's little Emily. She wants to see me. Colleen wants to see me!" Ian's voice lifted out of the fog of his mind. "My Colleen!"

Henry spoke for the first time. "No Ian, not Colleen. Colleen passed away..." He glanced at me. I supplied the answer.

"Two years ago. She passed away two years ago Ian. But Emily is alive. You're the only family she has left, and she wants to see you." I paused. "Do you want to see her?"

Ian's face was a writhing mask of emotion. He couldn't seem to decide how he felt. In a split second he was a raging fury, a picture of idyllic happiness and a mask of supreme sorrow. He finally settled on a perfectly blank expression.

"Emily. Yes."

I exhaled. "Ok, good. She's coming on Saturday with her aunt."

Ian's eyes were sharp again. "Joyce? She's coming here with Joyce?"

"She didn't say what her aunt's name was..."

"Joyce is Colleen's sister. A real shrew. She never liked me. Was always great with the kids though. She'll do. Saturday you said? That's tomorrow." He stood up with a quick, unfolding movement. "I need to clean up. Get the place ready for company." He turned suddenly towards Henry and me.

"How do I look?"

I looked at his scraggly, unwashed hair and his uneven beard. Henry ran his eyes over the purple sweatpants and red and black striped Rugby shirt and then glanced at me.

"Well," he said, "you could use some sprucing up."

Ian looked down at his ensemble and back up at us questioningly. "Maybe something in green?"

Henry stood up. "Tell you what, I'll go take a look in your closet and see what I can find. Is that ok?"

Ian nodded and looked to me. "What about you?"

I swallowed. "Maybe... a trim is in order?"

He ran his hands through his hair. "I don't have any scissors."

"That's ok, I brought some." I dumped out the contents of my bag. Scissors, a comb, and an electric razor fell out onto Fox's coffee table.

His face went bright red. "You. Brought. *Knives*. Into my *house?!*" He took a step forward.

I scooped them off the table into my lap and sputtered.

Fox let out a roar and dropped to a crouch in front of me. "First the papers. First the papers and the envelopes and then the questions about the picture and then my family yes my family and Colleen my Colleen and baby Emily and then it's knives knives and mirrors and reflections and memories that cut and knives—"

Henry's voice interrupted with a harsh briskness I'd never heard from him before. "Ian Fox! What kind of music do you like to listen to?"

Ian's ramblings broke off suddenly at this unexpected segue. He slowly looked up at Henry's slight frame that somehow seemed to tower over him.

"Music, Ian. What kind of music."

Fox scrunched his eyebrows together and then replied. "Blues."

Henry reached into his bag and pulled out a small portable stereo and set it on the table. He dug through a collection of CDs and pulled *King of the Delta Blues* by Robert Johnson. "Here's what we're going to do. I'm going to look in your closet for clothes. Jordan's going to trim your hair and beard. And you're going to listen to some blues. That's how we're going to get ready for Emily tomorrow. Ok?"

Ian thought about it, his lips twisted to the side. Then he nodded and sat down heavily on the coffee table, gesturing to me with one hand. "Chop-chop, Jordan."

Henry set the CD to play and walked out of the room and down the hall. We could hear him casually tossing aside hangers and digging through drawers. I thought Fox would have leapt up at the sound of his house being rummaged through, but he just sat in front me, listening to the buzz of the razor and humming along to the music.

Most of Ian's hair was too matted to cut with the razor I had brought, so I started with the school-supply scissors, sawing through thickened grease that was probably older than I was. Ian bathed, it would seem, but never got quite as far as cleaning his hair. At least I didn't see any lice.

I wasn't a whiz at hair styling, so I tried to play it safe. When I was finished, Ian's hair was at least even all the way around. It wasn't quite a buzz-cut, but it was pretty close. Then I went to work on the beard.

A cold shave with an electric razor isn't the most pleasant sensation when paired with thick, full facial hair, but Ian never complained. As I knelt in front of him, skimming the last few whiskers he looked me straight in the eye and said, "My daughter is coming over tomorrow you know."

I turned off the razor and dabbed his face with a cold, damp towel that Henry brought me. Ian's day-wear for tomorrow was all picked out and had been laid neatly across the couch.

Henry had chosen a simple pair of grey slacks and a white button-up shirt. It was *very* Henry. He shrugged my inquiring look away.

"There wasn't anything else, unless you want him in a crushed velvet smoking jacket and white jeans."

We left Ian with a few final reminders about personal hygiene and told him that we'd come get him tomorrow when Emily arrived. I was thrilled. The entire session had gone by without Ian mentioning the secret CD sale.

Henry had left the blues music playing as we exited the house.

"Music always helped my mother focus," he said as we walked past the mirrors. "I'm glad it worked for him too."

"I don't think Ian is bipolar. Or, at least, not *just* bipolar."

Henry shrugged in his twitchy way. "Maybe not, but the theory still stands."

I had a strange nervousness in the pit of my stomach. Henry felt it too, I could see. What if Fox was in bad shape tomorrow? What if Emily didn't show up? There were too many variables. I felt like a father standing outside the delivery room.

Henry saw the look on my face and laughed anxiously. "Well, good luck tomorrow."

"Yah. You too."

He walked past the fountain and entered his house. I looked across the way and noticed Jenny standing in her door, waving surreptitiously. I walked over.

"I had a brilliant idea, Jordan." Her eyes darted to Henry's house and back. "You know how we need Henry to be busy Sunday morning so we can set up for the sale? Well, Grace comes home from the hospital that day, so I thought I'd ask him to go pick her up. Do you think he'd do that if I asked him to?"

[123]

I think he'd do anything if you asked him to, I thought to myself. "I'm sure he would," I said. "You're right, that is a brilliant idea."

"Oh, he deserves this so much. And you're such a good friend to do it for him."

There was that word again. Friend. I didn't like the sound of it coming from her mouth.

Impulsively I reached out and touched her arm. She pulled away reflexively and bit her lip. "Sorry. I'm working on it." She looked up at me. "You're helping, you know."

I grinned. "Glad to be of service," I said as I swooped into a low bow.

As I righted myself, Jenny thrust herself forward and planted a kiss on my cheek. She fell back immediately with wide eyes, let out a short *squeak!*, and slammed the door between us.

I turned slowly on the spot until I was facing Henry's house.

Who's the Grand Master now?

As I slowly wandered through Grace's plaster menagerie towards my unit, I noticed Noah sitting in his white plastic chair by his front door, with Patton on his lap.

"Wasn't aware that Grace was back. Wasn't aware you were kissin' cousins either." His surly attitude did nothing to break my soaring heart.

"She's not back. For your information, that was Jenny." I shot him a look of triumph.

Noah leaned forward with sudden interest. "Jenny, you say? Pretty girl. Congratulations. But what's she doing in Grace's house when she's got her own just across the way?"

I explained about Jenny's sister. I wasn't surprised she hadn't told him yet. I bet shy Jenny went out of her way to avoid our gruff, grumpy complex manager.

Noah's eyes were alight. "So. Grace let her move in. That's just like her. Sweet and generous."

I blinked. *Sweet and generous?* "I thought she was a stubborn old battleaxe."

Noah looked up at me. "She's that too. A lesson, son. With women, you don't have to choose one or the other."

Patton snorted.

Dismissed.

Saturday, August 30

Saturday dawned bright and early. Brighter and earlier than I would have liked. The authoritarian pounding on my door woke me before 6:00.

Just when my alarm and I had come to an understanding, too.

It was Noah.

"Well, move aside. Or were you planning on making me hold this out here all day?"

He brushed past me, dragging an eight-foot long folding table into the house and leaning it against the hallway wall. He hurried back out and turned back to me.

"Step lively son. There are three more where that came from. And for all our sakes, put some damn clothes on. There are women out here."

I hurriedly ran back to my room and put on some jeans that were lying on my floor. Noah was laying the second table alongside the first when I joined him.

"Noah?" I ventured, "What are these tables for? And why are you putting them in my hallway?"

Noah looked at me incredulously. "I thought you said you were going to sell a bunch of music. Were you planning on stacking the albums on the ground in the mud?" He stomped back over the concrete to his unit, where two more tables were standing up against the wall. "What the hell kind of operation are you running here, son?"

I took one end of the table and let Noah guide me into my own home. He kept talking.

"Back in my day, we never used to do anything half-assed. All or nothing. Decision, action, and consequences. That's the way."

I smiled.

Noah noticed. "What's so funny?"

"Nothing. Grace told me you always said that."

"She did, eh? Seems to me you and Grace are pretty chummy. Hasn't shown you her bad side yet, has she? Stubborn old battleaxe."

We picked up the last table and headed towards my house. I rose to Grace's defence.

"Stubborn? Some would call it loyal."

Noah dropped the table with a hard *thunk*. "What did you just say?"

Belatedly, I realized I had overstepped my bounds.

"Loyal? What do you know about it? What *else* have you and Grace been talking about!?" Noah's voice rose in pitch and volume. "I will *not* be pitied!"

"I wasn't..." I dumped my reservations with my end of the table. My voice rose in concert with his. "We weren't even talking about you! We were talking about her brother, B—"

"DON'T YOU SAY HIS NAME!!" Noah's face took on an unhealthy shade of purple. "He was a damn fine man, a better man than you'll ever be! And you'd best still show some respect to me, boy, I've earned it!"

"I'll respect a man who does what he needs to do. Decision, action, consequences." I found myself stepping up to Noah and pointing my finger at his chest. "But I have no respect for a man that lets his personal doubts ruin someone else's happiness! Bill chose his life and Grace chose hers! By ending one you didn't need to end the other."

I breathed in deeply and shook my head. "I don't pity you. You pity yourself."

Noah stared at me hard, and didn't speak. His jaw worked in silence and his eyes glistened with anger. When he finally found his voice it was hard and cold.

"You have two more days left on your monthly lease. It won't be renewed. I expect you to live them quietly and then get out."

His door slammed shut behind him with booming finality.

I dragged the last table into my hallway, shut the door and leaned back against it, then slowly sank to the floor and put my head in my hands.

I spent the rest of the morning working on the music sale. I printed up price lists and made sure the other tenants had invited their friends. Louise and Sylvia promised to donate a collection of vinyl tablecloths and Jenny spent a few hours making a banner to hang from the speakers. As I was padding back and forth between the various units, I more than once saw Noah standing at his front window. His face was rock-hard. I hoped he didn't have any intention of making me cancel Henry's surprise. But he never stopped me. He just stood and watched.

At 11:30 I crossed over to Henry's place and sent him to make sure Ian was getting appropriately ready. Emily and her aunt would be here anytime. I went back home and put on a tie. It felt like a special occasion.

It was 11:56 when the knock came at my door. I invited Emily and her Aunt Joyce in and sat them down on the couch.

Emily took after her mother. She was about shoulder height to me with blond hair and blue eyes. I could a see strong resemblance in their facial features too, when I compared the girl in front of me to the woman in Ian's picture. She was sitting on the edge of the cushion, twisting her hands nervously and constantly glancing to her aunt for reassurance.

Emily's Aunt Joyce was a horse of a different colour. She was dark where Emily was pale and her dull brown eyes slowly and categorically took in my living room and dismissed it. She refused coffee and made a point of not speaking to me or to Emily in tacit disapproval of this entire event.

I took it upon myself as the host to make Emily as comfortable as possible.

"I'm glad you came."

She broke away from her intense study of the floor and put on her tough-guy face. "Yah, well, if this guy's into it then, whatever, right?"

Joyce frowned at her.

I stepped into the gap. "Well, this is a pretty big deal, for your dad and for you, I think." Emily looked at me warily. I was a stranger, after all.

"I'm just saying you shouldn't step into something like this with a 'whatever' attitude. It's important." I saw her roll her eyes, but her aunt broke in.

"That's exactly what I've been saying. This is not appropriate." She lifted her chin. I could tell she was just trying to protect her niece, but she came off imperious.

I interrupted. "That's not what I meant." Joyce sniffed, but I braved her icy look. "I just mean that your dad has put himself in a very vulnerable position by reaching out, and so have you."

"What are you, his therapist? Aren't you like, my age?"

I wanted to tell her I was one year older, but at that moment the front door opened. Henry had arrived with Ian.

Henry stepped into the living room first, his eyes taking in the two women sitting on my couch. He looked at me and raised his eyebrows.

I understood completely.

Here we go.

Henry stepped aside and Fox appeared in the doorframe. He was wearing the shirt and slacks that we had put out for him, his face was free of stubble, and his hair wasn't matted at all. Henry had been busy for the last 30 minutes.

"Ian," I said diplomatically, "this is your daughter, Emily. Emily, this is your father, Ian Fox." I stood from my chair and took one step back to give the Fox family the illusion of privacy. Henry remained behind Ian, and Joyce placed her hand on Emily's leg.

Emily stood up, all her false bravado gone. Her lip trembled.

"Dad?" She took one step forward. All eyes swung to Ian. It was his move.

He remained in the doorway. His eyes were confused. Emily shuffled her feet nervously.

Fox stared at Emily like the unenlightened look at a great piece of art; knowing there is beauty in the work, but unable to find it.

Ian's eyes began to flick back and forth between Emily and her aunt. The silence continued. I was just about to step in when Fox's face suddenly brightened in recognition.

"Joyce! You've brought her! You've brought her back to me!"

His daughter started to cry, a smile breaking across her features.

"My Colleen!"

Emily jerked back as if he had slapped her. Joyce gasped audibly.

"Colleen, you've come back! I've missed you! Did you bring baby Emily with you?"

Joyce stepped out in front of her niece. "We're leaving. This was a terrible idea." She began to pull Emily past Fox. He blocked her way.

"No! You can't take her again! I won't lose her again! Colleen!" Henry and I stepped in to hold Fox back. He was grabbing at Emily's arm, trying in vain to pull her from her aunt's grasp. Joyce opened the door and forcibly removed Emily from the house. For her part, Emily seemed in shock, not pressing to stay or seeking to go. She allowed herself to be directed towards the gate but kept looking over her shoulder at Fox, who was now standing in the doorframe weeping.

"My Colleen! They can't take her again! They can't take her again! She took my Emily!" He fell to his knees, sobbing. "She took my Emily."

At the sound of her name, Emily turned, but her aunt kept a firm grip on her arm and steered her out of the gate. I heard the sounds of a car door slamming twice, an engine turning over, and then a screech of tires and the rumble faded into the distance.

Fox was left on his knees, his white dress shirt stained with tears, Henry and I standing on either side of him like guardian angels. He wept softly to himself.

"Emily..."

Henry had taken Fox home and calmed him down. I stayed sitting in my living room for hours. This had been a disastrous day. I was pretty sure that Noah wasn't allowed to evict me just because I'd fought with him, but I didn't want to be the next-door neighbour of a man who hated me. It would be hard to leave the rest of them though. Even Fox. I had grown attached to him, idiosyncrasies and all. I only hoped he could forgive me for this afternoon's debacle.

The phrase "The road to hell is paved with good intentions" flashed through my mind. At least it was over.

There was a knock at the door. Two sharp raps.

Louise and Sylvia.

Damn.

I'd forgotten that it was Saturday. Tonight we break into the school. I turned the knob. "Come in."

They trooped in the door dressed in their blacks with fabric slippers overtop of their shoes. Sylvia eyed my tie with disdain.

"Go change your clothes. This is the big one."

We packed our gear into the rear of the wagon. I kept a sharp eye out for Inspector Longstaff, but there were too many darkened cars parked out on the street. No one seemed to be watching.

While Louise pulled away from the curb and started carefully down the road, I took the opportunity to remind both sisters of my feelings about tonight's little escapade.

"They're setting a trap for us. I know it."

Sylvia snorted. "No one is setting a trap for us. Cool your jets, Jesse James."

Louise nodded in agreement but I noticed she kept glancing in the rear-view mirror.

We pulled into the school parking lot at 7:15 PM. There were no other vehicles in sight. Louise parked the car and we all slipped out into the night.

I started to pull the sledgehammer from the back, but Louise stopped me.

"Not tonight, Jordan. It's just a punching bag, remember?" She flipped a blanket to cover the hammer and we walked towards the school, slipping on our latex gloves.

We saw nothing suspicious on the grounds as we circled the building until we reached the gymnasium side-door. It was sitting slightly ajar.

My eyes grew wide. "Someone's already been here."

Louise looked at Sylvia and they both nodded. Sylvia whispered back to me. "Or they might still be here." She clicked on a flashlight and slowly pulled open the door.

The vast space of the empty gymnasium felt deepened by the blackness that filled it. We stepped cautiously through the darkness, following the wall and guided only by the jerky beam of Sylvia's flashlight. She paused every few feet and motioned for quiet. Hearing nothing, she would then continue on. We crossed the room in perfect silence in under a minute, but it seemed like an eternity.

We reached the far wall. Sylvia's flashlight had just found the door marked "Equipment Storage" when Louise stiffened suddenly behind me. We all froze and that's when I heard it.

A shuffling sound. And some muttering.

It was coming from inside the equipment room.

"Someone's in there." My voice felt croaky in my throat, though it came out in a hushed whisper. Sylvia gave me a look that told me I never again need to state the obvious in her presence, and mouthed the words, *thanks, Baby Bear.* She motioned towards the door leading to the school proper. We tiptoed as quickly as we could across the gym floor and passed through an inner door, letting it close silently behind us.

I paused and let out a deep breath before I looked up to address the sisters. "Who do you think—?"

I broke off. The sisters were gone. Well, not gone, but they were racing down the hallway, their slippers making hushed flapping sounds as they ran. Louise looked over her shoulder and wildly beckoned me.

I've never been much of a runner, but I sprinted down that hallway with a speed that would have put an Olympic champion to shame.

We jimmied the lock on another side-door and stepped out into the cool night air. I just had time to wonder why no alarms were going off, what with all these opened doors, when I noticed that again, neither Sylvia nor Louise had stopped moving. They were halfway to the car already and I hurried to catch up. We got in the car and were out on the road in moments. I heard both sisters breathe a sigh of relief as the school faded into the distance.

We were about five minutes away from home when the flashing lights appeared in our rear-view.

"Remain calm." Sylvia advised from behind her clenched teeth. "We've done nothing wrong."

That seemed to me to be a gross distortion of reality.

A tap on the window instructed Louise to roll it down, and behind a bright flashlight I saw the face of Inspector Longstaff appear. The haunting light in his hand and the rotating blue and red emanating from the roof of his vehicle enhanced the sickly look of his face. For the first time, he truly frightened me.

"Step out of the car please." His flashlight crossed over into the backseat and found me trembling there. "All of you."

We were herded to the hood of his patrol car by his partner, a heavyset woman he called Pat. She had us place our hands on the hood and spread our legs. I've always imagined being frisked by a female police officer would be an interesting experience.

I was right, but not in the way I had wanted to be.

When she had finished, Longstaff sent her to search the station wagon. Neither Louise nor Sylvia said a word. Out of the corner of my eye I saw Sylvia set her face, her mouth twisted into a morbid grin.

Game time.

Longstaff paced slowly behind us.

"So, what are you three doing out here at this time of night?"

Sylvia answered. "This time of night? It's 7:30. We—"

Longstaff interrupted. "I was asking Jordan."

I swallowed nervously and glanced to my left. Louise gave me a wink.

A wink? We were being arrested, and she winked at me? I looked at Sylvia on my right. Her smile had broadened.

And suddenly I realized. They had nothing on us. We weren't at the scene. We hadn't touched the money. We hadn't left any fingerprints because of the gloves. Longstaff was trying to scare me into a confession that I didn't have to make. Hell, this time I didn't even have anything to confess! I broke into a broad grin.

"I'm waiting, Jordan. Why are you out here?"

"We just came out for a walk, Inspector. Nothing like the crisp autumn air, don't you agree?"

"Are you trying to be funny, Melville? 'Cause I'm not laughing."

I bit back a dozen snide replies. "No sir."

"Does this look like a nice area for walking, Melville?"

I looked around us. We had been pulled over in an industrial area. A large abandoned warehouse loomed over an all-night pawn shop across the street. The pawn shop's staff and customers were gawking out the window at us.

"No it doesn't, sir."

"Then why were you walking here?"

"We weren't walking here. We were driving here. You just pulled us over, remember?" I felt Sylvia nudge me gently. *Careful, Jordan...don't push him too far.*

"Don't get smart with me kid. I followed you from your complex tonight, you know. All the way to that nice little elementary school. What were you doing at an elementary school, Jordan? Decide university was too good for you after all?"

I'd had a long day, and this guy was starting to piss me off. "I told you, going for a walk. The playing field is a nice flat space for speed-walking." I felt Louise trying to hold in a laugh. I was warming up to my subject.

"We go every Friday. Just to stretch our legs. Exercise is good for the brain."

Longstaff didn't like having his own *bon mots* tossed back at him.

"Just to stretch your legs, eh? Well, I had a few of my men stretch their legs there tonight as well, and do you know what we found?"

I couldn't resist. "An unfit police force?"

Sylvia laughed out loud. Longstaff grabbed my shoulder and spun me around, pinning me to the hood of his car with his forearm. "A robbery in progress. You wouldn't know anything about that now, would you?"

Louise spoke before I could deny everything. "You said a robbery in progress, did you not?"

Longstaff didn't look away from my face. His lip was curled cruelly and his eyes were bulging out. He nodded.

Sylvia joined in. "But that means you found a thief. Caught in the act."

Longstaff blinked. "That's what my men tell me." He was starting to look unsure of himself.

Louise turned her head towards him. "Then if you've caught someone, why are you bothering us? We're innocent bystanders—"

Sylvia took up the chase. "The subjects of police harassment—"

"Who are, quite frankly, getting fed up."

Longstaff's head had swivelled between them as they spoke. He looked back down at me, confusion written all over his face.

[133]

"But you were there. It all fit."

I shrugged from my position atop the hood. "I hardly believe it myself."

He roughly pulled me from the car. "If I find out that you're playing me—"

"Paul. Take a look at these." Longstaff's partner Pat was standing near the rear of the station wagon, holding up a sledgehammer and three sets of latex gloves. He spun back to us and roared.

"Ha! What do you call that!"

Sylvia leaned forward and spoke as dryly as I'd ever heard her speak. "Circumstantial."

Louise draped her arm protectively around my shoulder. Sylvia took my hand and started us walking back to the car. Longstaff stood in the strobing lights of his patrol car with a singularly defeated look on his face. Pat looked at him, then at us, unsure of what to do with all her new-found evidence. Louise started the car and began to pull away as Sylvia rolled her window down and looked out at Pat.

"Keep 'em."

We peeled away from the curb.

Our laughter filled the car as we drove home. The look on Longstaff's face when he finally understood that he had nothing on me would stay with me for the rest of my life, I was sure. We pulled up to the gate at Stony Creek Estates and made our way to 5A.

Once inside, Louise headed to the kitchen to make some tea and Sylvia sat down in her chair. I took a spot on the couch and as Louise came in with the tea and biscuits and made herself comfortable, I realized that these were the same seats we'd sat in one and a half weeks ago when the Gordon sisters offered me a job. My curiosity finally got the best of me.

"Why me?"

Louise looked up from her biscuits. "Pardon?"

I repeated myself. "Why me? You didn't even know me. I could've turned you in, I could've blown your cover. You have such a racket going, what do you need me for?

Sylvia set her plate down. She looked at me with an unnerving fondness. "You asked us that the first day too."

"I remember." I said. "And I remember your answer. *That is exactly the point.* And I still don't understand what you meant."

"What I meant was we shouldn't need you." She folded her hands in her lap. "Jordan, you're right. Louise and I had a good thing going. But there was one thing wrong. Someone was catching on."

I could guess. "The warden."

Louise nodded. "George had told us he was going to tape our next session. We had Tom sing, of course. But we knew that if the warden somehow got the information—"

"He'd be able to send the police around to do some serious digging."

I struggled to follow along. "But they didn't have any evidence."

Sylvia shrugged. "Wouldn't matter. They'd find some, soon enough." Her eyes sparkled. "You like CSI. You should know. *There's always evidence.*"

Louise smiled. "So, when you moved in, looking all fresh-faced and innocent—"

"We decided to deal you in."

"We figured, what cop would ever look at two middle-aged women—"

"When an 18-year old boy is a suspect too?"

My mouth dropped open. "I was bait?"

Sylvia nodded happily. "50,000 dollars worth of bait."

"And worth every penny." Louise grunted. "You were wonderful."

"With you running around, your fingers in so many pies—"

"The police didn't even see us. I have a suspicion that Inspector Longstaff thought you used *us* as cover, instead of the other way around!"

"Of course, there were complications." Sylvia sipped her tea.

"Yah," I said, still stinging from the revelation. "Longstaff figured out I was opening all the mail."

"Actually," Louise cleared her throat, "We may have helped him along to that conclusion."

"What?!" I jumped up from the couch, nearly dumping my tea. "You ratted me out? After I kept all your secrets?"

Sylvia frowned and wiped a spot of tea from her sleeve. "Calm down, Jordan. The more he watched you, the easier it was for us to make plans."

I sat down sulkily. "What plans?"

Louise beamed. "Why, tonight's trap of course!"

I burst out again. "Trap! You told me that no one was setting a trap!"

"Actually, what I said was, no one is setting a trap *for us*. You see, we were the ones setting the trap." Sylvia leaned back in silence and regarded me over the lip of her cup just like she'd done when we'd first started down this road.

I sat in confusion for a moment before it came to me. "The warden! That was the warden at the school!"

Louise clapped her hands. "Very good, Jordan!" She gave me a biscuit.

Sylvia looked pleased as well. "It was the tape that gave it away."

I was lost again. "What tape?"

"The tape that Warden Goodman released to the police with our names and voices on it."

"But, he never released the tape." I rubbed my temple.

"Exactly." Louise rattled her cup in the saucer. "And why not? If he wanted us stopped he could have done it once he knew what we were up to. But he didn't."

I was slowly catching up. "But he still sent the patrol car to the apartment that night. Why bother if he didn't want us caught?"

"To prove his theory. My guess is he made an anonymous tip to the police just to see if we had been there. He must have connections at the department. It would be easy enough for him to find out what had happened at the scene."

I slowly continued the thought. "So when he heard that the walls were knocked in and there were empty bags on the bed—"

"Along with the money we left to cover the damages—" Louise interjected.

"He knew he was on the right track." Sylvia finished.

"He didn't want to catch you." I'd finally got it. "He wanted to use you. To get—"

"The money." All three of us concluded in unison.

We all took a sip of our tea. Most of mine had sprayed onto my lap during my outburst and what was left had gone cold. Sylvia volunteered to top us up. She took all of our cups into the kitchen. I finish the unravelling myself.

"So, it *was* a trap tonight. A trap for the warden."

Louise nodded.

"Why didn't you tell me?"

She smiled again. "Because you were so very innocent, but seemed so very guilty. Your natural nervousness was much more believable than if we'd told you and you'd been faking it."

Sylvia called out from the kitchen. "And you were terrific! When you said 'an unfit police force,' I almost died!"

The flattery helped, but I wasn't finished.

"Ok, fine. How about this? Was there really ten million dollars in the bag?"

Sylvia came back in and sat down, handing the cups out. "No. Only one million. We had to make if big enough that he'll get serious jail time, but we didn't want to throw good money away."

I had another question. "So who was that monster in the jail then? The one who oh-so-conveniently told us the place, date, and time?"

Louise smiled her biggest smile. "That was Darrell. Darrell Feltzner."

That was not a name I'd have expected to belong to that monstrous gorilla.

"He's our cousin—"

"Second cousin—"

"Once removed."

"Quite a performance, wasn't it?"

In hindsight, the family resemblance was obvious.

"And Goodman didn't know?" I was a little surprised.

"As far as I know, he never looked into it! Blinded by greed, I suppose. The man's an idiot. Tom was even able to make excuses for his singing in the visitor's room and get away with it."

They sat back in their chairs, basking in the glow of a job well done.

But I had one final question. "What do you do with the money? You can't take 2.5 million dollars to the bank and make a cash deposit."

"That's true. We do put our business partner's money into banks all over the world, just like we promise. But we're stuck with our cut. So we store it up and make small deposits every two weeks." For once in her life Sylvia had the grace to look sheepish. "The government seems to be under the impression that we own a small hardware store."

[137]

My mind flew through the statistics. "But you've been doing this for over 30 years. Where can you store that much money?" I had visions of cellar doors guarded by skeletons; the walls lined with gold bullion flickering in torchlight.

Louise looked at Sylvia.

Sylvia looked at Louise.

They both nodded. "He's come this far," said Sylvia.

They rose to their feet.

"Come with us."

I led the way out the front door. I had reached the fountain before I realized that there were no footsteps behind me. I turned slowly to see Louise and Sylvia standing in front of unit 4B.

No.

Way.

I stormed up to the sisters. Louise had a key in the door.

"No. Not possible. Noah told me this was unused." The key clicked in the lock.

Sylvia raised her right eyebrow. "I think if you remember back, you'll find he probably told you it was vacant. Not unused. There is a world of difference."

We stepped into unit 4B and Sylvia locked the door behind us. I stood aside as the pair of them rumbled down the hallway looking as if they were about to board the ark. I followed them past the empty living room, bedroom, and kitchen to the second bedroom at the end of the hall. They turned and walked to the closet. Each of them took hold of one door and opened it slowly in the manner of Imperial Guards.

It was empty.

Except for the trapdoor installed in the floor.

I looked up at Louise. "But my house doesn't have a crawlspace. And all the houses are the same." I turned to Sylvia. "Right?"

She just smiled and motioned towards the trapdoor. I moved forward and lifted it. It revealed a set of carpeted stairs leading down into blackness. Louise reached around me and flicked a switch. The lights came on, and I stepped down...

... into a carbon copy of the upper floor.

It wasn't a crawlspace.

It was another house, reversed so that I was once again standing in the front hallway. But no one lived in this unit.

There wasn't room.

Every wall was lined with shelves, and every shelf held money. In the subterranean living room tote bags, cardboard boxes, and briefcases bowed the shelves with their weight, I even saw one flamingo-shaped piggybank. The shelves stretched all the way down the hallway as well. I wandered the rooms while the sister's stood with their backs to the closed front door. I saw money of every denomination. The entire second bedroom had been set aside for coins only. The kitchen housed foreign currency. There were millions of dollars here.

I returned to the staircase. "This is unbelievable! There's no way you could have built this without people noticing!"

Sylvia grunted. "There was a two week period in 1982. Noah was away on an all-expenses paid cruise that we had set up for him."

Louise smiled. "Contractors can move awfully quickly when properly motivated."

I looked up at the two most formidable women I'd ever met. "And everyone else?"

Sylvia helped me up the stairs. "Oh, we passed around the word that Noah was fixing some issue or another so he could try to rent it. No one else here knows that *we* rent it." She sighed, "You don't seem to understand, Jordan. Before you moved in, we all pretty much kept to ourselves."

Louise led the way back to the front door, and as she locked it behind us I noticed something.

There was no sign of a security system.

I ran my hands through my hair. "This is crazy! What if someone finds it! What if a thief finds out! You could lose everything!"

Sylvia shrugged. "There's plenty more where that came from."

Louise bobbed her head. "Finding it is the fun part anyway."

I couldn't think of anything else to say.

So I laughed.

Sunday, August 31

I forgot to set my alarm. I woke up at 11:02 to a banging on my door. I stumbled down the hall and wondered why Noah had never installed doorbells in these units.

At the door was the delivery man from the sound system rental company. He had already unloaded the equipment and as I signed for them I noticed Noah near the fountain, straining to attach the speakers to the large stands. The delivery man wheeled his dolly back out the gate.

I was still uncomfortable with Noah. After all, I had disrespected him, and he had evicted me. But I wasn't about to let a man in his late-80s lift four 14 kg speakers onto six foot poles by himself. I put on some pants and went out to help him.

His face screwed up in a scowl as I took the second speaker from him. Neither of us spoke as we set it in place. As soon as the last speaker was up, completing the square of sound that we'd set around the fountain, Noah shuffled back to his unit and closed the door.

At least he was still helping, and not shutting me down.

I noticed Jenny waving at me from Grace's house. I walked over and she stepped out of the door. "Henry took a cab to get Grace about 20 minutes ago. He just missed the speakers arriving! I stole his glasses so he wouldn't see the flyers. And I sent a note with him for Grace." She giggled. "I told her to slow him down as much as she could to give us time, and get here just after 12:00."

I took Henry's glasses from her outstretched hand.

"You little criminal!" Jenny blushed. I liked her in red. "Perfect. Now I just have to go set everything up."

"Oh, I had one more idea. I saw some cookie recipes in Grace's kitchen, and... do you think she'd mind if I made some and we sold them too?"

I beamed at her, proud. Maybe she wouldn't come out into the crowd today. But she was getting involved, and getting involved was a big step for her.

"I think that's a great idea. Grace will love it."

I turned back out to the courtyard. Fox was standing by the fountain, fiddling with the portable soundboard and CD player that had come with the speaker system. I rushed out, watching my security deposit disappear before my eyes, and then froze as *King of the Delta Blues* began to issue from the speakers. Fox fiddled with some dials until the output was perfectly adjusted. Robert Johnson proclaimed *I'm a Steady Rollin' Man* to the entire complex, and the sharp *zzzing* of guitar strums rebounded around the courtyard in crystal clarity. Ian sat on the ring of the fountain, bobbing his head and clapping his hands against his legs in time to the music.

I'd never thought to wonder what he did in his life. For some reason it was his dark afterlife that had interested me the most. Now I bet it had something to do with music.

Ian would've made a great roadie.

I left him to his business and went to retrieve the four tables from my hallway. As I was setting them up I saw Noah stooping over the wires running from the sound equipment to an outdoor electrical socket between 2A and 3A.

He noticed me watching him and stood up with a defiant look on his face.

"I'm not about to have someone trip and sue me for every penny I've got just so that you can have a block party." He went back to securing the wires with twine.

And he wasn't the only one getting involved. The smell of cookies began to waft from Jenny and Grace's unit. Louise and Sylvia turned up with the promised tablecloths and a coin box for change and then used their height to hang the banner Jenny had made yesterday.

[141]

In bright green paint across an old bed-sheet were the words,

Henry Davidson
by Henry Davidson,

surrounded by a few copies of the flyer I'd printed off.

Jenny had even used packing tape to secure a CD case to the sheet. *Transient Sunlight* beamed across the courtyard. As marketing strategies go it was simple, but effective.

Fox had run back to his house when he saw the banner go up and now returned to us wearing his blond handlebar moustache with pride. He was also carrying a roll of aluminum foil, which he proceeded to wrap around the speaker poles, possibly to keep any governmental or alien subliminal messaging from being inserted into the music.

I got the boxes of CDs from my spare room, and Louise quietly and professionally broke into Henry's house for the original shipment. She began to display them in stacks on the tablecloths while Sylvia started up the old BBQ for the first time since 1974. She'd obviously planned to do this, since she was using a shiny new propane tank and sitting in a cooler next to her was an assortment of frozen burgers, pops, and beers.

I noticed that this allowed her to stand guard unobtrusively near 4B.

People started to arrive at quarter to twelve, and flowed in steadily. Fox switched the CD over to Henry's, and his clear tenor voice floated above the courtyard and out into the neighbourhood, drawing in passing by pedestrians and traffic. I started taking cash almost immediately.

Most of the crowd were strangers, but many of them were familiar faces to me. I saw Grace's nurse Rebekah, who'd taken the day off, wandering through the wind-chimes decorating 3B. Sasha must have gotten the flyer and passed it on, because Professor Hender rolled in just before noon and took up a permanent station near the BBQ. Even Tom and George from the prison had made it out. Their faces melded in and out of the crowd, but at least twice I saw Tom standing in the centre of a small group, adding a harmony line to Henry's masterful voice.

And then I saw a face I didn't expect.

Standing at the gate, being passed on both sides by people coming and going, was Emily Tremont.

She had hidden her blond hair underneath a hat, and her face was hidden behind a pair of sunglasses. She was twisting her hands like she had been yesterday, staring into the crowd. I followed her line of sight and saw Ian, standing surrounded by strangers. He was doing card tricks.

I walked down to the gate. Aunt Joyce was nowhere to be found.

"Hey."

"Hey," she said back. She looked up at me and blurted out, "I want to apologize. I was such a jerk to you when you were just trying to help my dad. I feel terrible. It's not your fault that it... turned out like it did."

I told her no apology was necessary.

"No, it is. It wasn't until we were leaving that I realized you were right. I need my dad more than I thought I did." Her eyes drifted back over to Fox. "I saw the flyer as we were driving away yesterday. I thought... maybe if I came back... and didn't look so much like my mom..." Her hand went unconsciously to her hat. "Maybe I can just be one of the crowd. Maybe talk to him a bit. You know? Like, casual?"

I thought it was brilliant, and said so. Emily placed her hand on my arm and squeezed.

"Thanks Jordan." She vanished into the crowd around Fox and I soon heard her laughing in delight as he guessed her card.

Ten minutes later I heard a car door slam.

Henry had arrived.

He entered through the gates of Stony Creek, with Grace on his arm and a look of shocked bewilderment on his face. I ran up to him and presented him with his glasses.

"Surprise!"

He slipped his glasses on and took in the scene around him. Grace stood beside him, marvelling at the size of the crowd, her eyes landing on each resident individually, noting their presence and contributions.

She smiled up at me with a teacher's satisfaction. After all, she'd started me down this road. "Well done Jordan. I knew you could do it."

I just about burst with pride.

The crowd began to cheer and call out Henry's name.

"Bravo!"

"Well done Henry!"

"It's just beautiful, Henry! I love it!"

Grace slipped her arm through mine and we followed Henry as he slowly made his way through the crowd, receiving praise for his work and pats on the back as he went.

It was Henry-mania.

But he still hadn't responded to a single congratulatory remark when he arrived at the fountain. He stopped and took in the tables, now mostly free of his CDs. He saw the banner and the flyers. He saw Fox doing magic on one side of the courtyard and Sylvia burning patties on the other. Louise and Noah were manning the tables, Louise munching on a snickerdoodle that had just come out of Grace's oven and zealously guarding the cashbox while Noah was sipping on a beer and keeping an eagle eye out for litterbugs. Jenny waved at us from her doorway.

Henry remained perfectly silent.

A call rang out. "Encore!"

The crowd picked it up.

"Sing something for us Henry!"

"Oh please!"

"Sing!"

Henry lifted his head to the sky, turned, and walked silently into his house.

I exchanged looks with Jenny. That was not according to plan. Had we embarrassed him with all this attention? Jenny looked like she was about to cry, and turned back into her house. A muted hum buzzed from the crowd. I could pick out fragments.

"Well, that wasn't very gracious..."

"I've half a mind to ask for my money back..."

"What happened to his moustache?"

As awkward conversation broke out again and filled the courtyard, I moved to take Grace to her house. Noah eased up out of his chair and blocked our way.

He had a very ugly and self-satisfied smile on his face.

"So you're back."

Grace smiled up at him sweetly. "You don't think you could get rid of me that easily, do you? I'm not going anywhere for a while, Noah Foster, so you'd best just get used to me."

Noah cocked his head and his grin widened. "I wouldn't be so sure if I were you. Melville here tells me that you've let the Dryden girl move into your unit. I assume she'll be paying you some rent for her room?"

Grace nodded. "And I'm glad to be able to do it. That girl needs someone just like I do."

The look on Noah's face solidified into granite. "Well Grace, I'm afraid that constitutes an unauthorized sub-let." I wasn't following, but Grace's face went white and she began trembling on my arm. "That's grounds for eviction, Grace." Noah chuckled. "I can finally get you out of my hair."

I steadied myself, expecting to have to support Grace's weight. But she surprised me. She stepped out of my grasp and up to Noah. The noise of the crowd around them seemed to fade away.

Grace placed her hand on his chest. "Oh, Noah. After all these years." She looked up at him, her face pale, her eyes desperate. "Is this how it will end?"

Noah stood stiffly in front of her. He didn't move her hand from his chest. He didn't move at all. All you could see was the rise and fall of Grace's hand as Noah took steady, shallow breaths. Their eyes were locked together and neither of them spoke for a moment. I waited to see Noah's face soften, but it didn't come. The hard look in his eyes remained unchanged as he reached up his hand to remove hers.

But when he touched her, something happened. The rigid lines of his face cracked. A single tear broke through the reserve of his features and he simply placed his hand on hers. "Well then," he croaked. "You'd best make sure she pays you on time, because rent day is still the same, no matter how many of you live in the house."

Grace's smile burst out into the open, her laugh lines creating troughs for her tears. She leaned her head up against Noah's chest and he enveloped her in his arms.

"You stubborn old fool."

Noah smiled. "You testy old battleaxe."

He caught me staring at them. "What is it, Melville? Enjoying the show?" He lifted a hand from Grace's back and pointed it at my face. "Just because you like to waltz around in your underwear doesn't mean everyone else can't appreciate a little privacy."

I turned away and smiled.

And saw a sight to behold. There, standing framed in his doorway, was Henry.

He was dressed in an immaculate tuxedo, he had slicked his hair back, and he was wearing a wide, black cape.

I laughed out loud. *I knew he had a cape!*

The murmuring of the crowd turned to exclamations as they started to notice him, and soon cheers rang though the courtyard once more.

Henry acknowledged them with a slight bow of his head and slowly and dramatically made his way through the crowd to the fountain. He stepped up on the edge and flipped his cape over his arm. At a nod, Fox shut off the sound system. Henry closed his eyes for a moment and a hush fell over the crowd.

He took a deep breath and began to sing.

The first strains of *Nessun Dorma* wafted over his audience, gently pushing from our ears all other sound. Shuffling footsteps were stilled, traffic ceased to flow, the birds hushed. All that existed in the world was Henry's voice. I looked around the crowd. Louise and Sylvia stood next to one another with their eyes closed. Noah still held Grace and they rocked back and forth as the notes swept their past away.

Henry's voice swelled.

The crowd was unmoving. Even Fox was still. He was listening to the music, but his eyes were fixed on Emily, who was kneeling beside him. She had taken off her sunglasses, and Fox slowly reached out and removed her hat. Her blonde hair fell cascading past his hand, and he brushed the tears from her face. *Emily*, I saw him mouth. She took his hand and he pulled her close.

Finally I turned to see Jenny. She stood in the doorway, entranced.

I looked at her face and knew I'd just lost the battle for her heart.

As Henry approached the towering climax of the piece, Jenny's face began to glow. The fearful paleness that so often clouded her cheeks melted away. She was slowly stepping forward from the door as he progressed. He reached the final note and it exploded through the courtyard, relieving the audience of its breath. The note seemed to soar away long after Henry had let it go and no one dared to speak, or even move, as it slowly dissipated like an early morning fog.

Jenny was the first to break the stillness. She darted out the door and across the courtyard, threw herself at a very unprepared Henry, and kissed him squarely on the mouth.

The crowd roared its approval.

Henry stood in shock for a moment before he realized what was happening. He then wrapped his arms around her and kissed her passionately in return.

Check and mate.

I felt Grace's hand on my arm and looked down at her face. She reached up and patted my shoulder. "Better luck next time, Jordan."

I smiled down at her as she returned to Noah. I was ok. I didn't blame Jenny. Hell, if he'd held the note for one more second *I'd* have kissed him. Along with everyone else in the crowd.

The music's spell was broken. Henry stepped down with Jenny clinging to his arm, surrounded by all the things she feared most in the world, but able to stand tall at the side of the man she loved.

Sylvia fired up the BBQ and Grace manned the cookie table, directly underneath the first speaker. I recalled the day I moved in, when Grace warned me not to play my music too loudly. She didn't seem to mind today. Noah was standing behind her and caught my eye with a heavy glare.

Louise took over CD sales, was out of stock in minutes, and began feverishly taking orders that would be filled by the third shipment scheduled to arrive next Friday. Fox sat on the fountain with Emily, teaching her how to pull the ace of spades.

I wandered through the crowd, basking in my handiwork, enjoying what was probably going to be the last enjoyable moment I spent living with these people.

Tomorrow was September 1st. Orientation at university started bright and early and as of now, I had no place to live while attending.

I made my way over to the BBQ, where I caught the tail end of a conversation between Sylvia and Tom, the prison guard.

"Yup, it was Goodman all right. Caught him with his hand right in the bag they said. Turns out they'd been after him for a while, only they didn't know it. He'd been running his own operation for years. Inspector fellow that came to the jail to interview us all told me he called himself the Peruvian Banker. Said his mother was born in Lima."

Sylvia's right eyebrow rose in surprise. She hadn't expected that.

Tom continued, unawares. "Whoda thunk it? Of course, I never liked him. He told me my Pirate King was pitchy."

The sun was setting by the time the crowds were gone. Fox's mirrors caught the evening light and spread dusk around the courtyard in fractured shards. Emily had left, giving me her phone number on the way out the gate. She'd wanted me to call her up for coffee sometime. I had put the paper in my pocket and thought of Jenny kissing Henry.

I wasn't ready to call Emily yet.

But tomorrow is another day.

Behind me, Noah and the Gordon sisters had packed away the tables and sound equipment and gone back into their units. Henry was at Jenny's house wishing her and Grace a good night. They closed the door and he strolled over to the fountain, looking at a leftover flyer that had fallen inside. I walked up beside him and we stood there, staring into the dry pool.

Henry spoke first.

"Nice party."

"Nice cape."

He raised his eyebrow. "You don't like it?"

I smiled. "I think it would go well with the moustache."

Henry chuckled and looked over at Jenny's door.

"So... no hard feelings then?"

I reached out and shook his hand. "No hard feelings. I don't think I could ever compete with a genius caped superhero."

Henry looked at me in mock concern. "Oh come on. You have strengths. How about those Superman boxers, eh?"

I laughed. He raised an eyebrow.

"Besides, I saw you standing with Emily for awhile. She's cute."

"Back off poindexter. I saw her first."

Henry clapped me on the back and sobered. "Seriously though, Jordan, thanks for all this." His arm swept around the courtyard. "You're a true friend."

As he wandered back to his unit, sweeping his cape in the air like a nerdy little Dracula, I realized that the F-word was growing on me.

I turned back towards my unit and saw a figure standing in the shadows by my door. It stepped forward.

It was Inspector Longstaff.

"So... we meet again, eh Jordan?" His gaunt face was twisted in a sneer. "I don't know how you pulled it off, but you did it. Congratulations. Not just anyone can get away with such a masterful performance." He advanced towards me, clapping slowly in false appreciation.

"But you know what I've found out about criminals, Jordan? They always make one little mistake." He stepped around behind me and spoke into my ear. "They got Al Capone for tax evasion."

He circled back around in front of me and stopped. "I'll tell you a secret, Jordan. I'm not a well man." He looked it. "In fact, starting next week I'm going on medical leave for a while. Who knows for how long? And all I wanted before I went was one more big bust. And then you showed up."

Longstaff threw his hands up in the air. "Hallelujah! A genuine multi-million dollar case falls into my lap. But I made the mistake of underestimating you because... You're. So. Young!" He spit out the last three words.

"And you outsmarted me. Made me look the fool. Sure, we got the guy, but he wasn't you, was he, Jordan?" I didn't respond. I just stared straight ahead. "Nope. You got off scot-free. Except for one thing." Longstaff clapped his hands loudly together in triumph.

"You pulled a Capone! Millions of dollars, free and clear, and you made the *stupid* mistake of opening your neighbours' mail."

The blood drained from my face. Longstaff saw it and his sneer widened.

"Oh yes. That's a federal offence, Superman. I may not be able to get you for the money, but I'll sure as hell get you for the mail!" His voice rose in victory and a pair of silver handcuffs appeared in his hands.

"Good evening, Inspector Longstaff." The voice came out of nowhere. Both Longstaff and I peered around for the source. I found it first.

Standing outside the door of 2A was a figure. It was tall and thin, wrapped in a full length coat with fur edging. It was standing directly in front of the porch light and its face was obscured in shadow.

It was Sasha.

Sasha's voice had a rusty gravel to it. It carried a vague accent I couldn't place. South African, or maybe Serbian. It spoke again.

"I'm surprised to see you out and about tonight, what with tomorrow being such an important day for you. Is there any way my young friend here can help you? Or has my Iranian friend helped you enough already?"

Longstaff's already hollow face had fallen in on itself. The handcuffs vanished into a pocket as he backed away from me. "No, Sterling. I don't need anything else." He turned towards the gate.

Sasha spoke with firmness, "Good evening, Inspector Longstaff. And good luck tomorrow."

Longstaff disappeared around the corner with a sour twist to his mouth and a sheen of sweat on his forehead.

Sasha's head turned, and I thought I saw a smile form on slight lips in the shadow.

"I hope Inspector Longstaff enjoys his new kidney." The porch light flicked off. "Good night, Jordan."

I stood in the vacant courtyard, staring in awe at the fading silhouette of Sasha Sterling; black market profiteer, collector of odd antiquities, invisible and indefinable. Until now.

My saviour.

I realized then that I'd been wrong about my neighbours all along; they were never crazy.

I had always been just a little too sane.

Monday, September 1

The alarm went off at 7:30 AM, precisely. I rolled out of bed.

Even though it was technically Labour Day, the Student Union had chosen to offer optional orientation for first-years. That meant that today was my first day of school. It was also my last day as a resident of Stony Creek Estates. I had a quick shower and cup of coffee and headed out the door, grabbing my registration papers on the way. I had one final thing to do before I left.

I knocked on Noah's door.

He opened it with a surly, "What."

I took a deep breath. I'd rehearsed this. "Noah, I want to apologize for what I said on Saturday. It was extremely rude and disrespectful and I shouldn't have said it."

Noah pursed his lips and stared at me. My fate was on the line.

In my head, this conversation went one of two ways. Either Noah refused my apology and I ran from the gate with Patton chewing on my leg, or he tearfully accepted it and apologized himself, making us fast friends.

"Fine." Noah moved to close the door.

"Wha- what?" I stammered. I dropped my papers in surprise. This was not going according to plan.

"I said fine. A sincere apology is all a man can ask for. You can stay. But just you watch your tone around me, son. Is that clear?"

"Yes sir."

"Good, now pick up your mess and get out." Same old Noah. Always the gracious host.

I bent down and scooped up the registration papers. One was missing. I looked up and saw Patton turn the corner into his room with my paperwork in his mouth. Noah glanced down the hallway where I was looking and sighed.

"Alright, go get it. Double-time now."

I hurried down the hall and turned into Patton's room. His bed sat in the centre of the otherwise empty floor. Patton's bed was a tiny replica of Fox's hallway. It had been turned into a nest, full of scraps of paper; newsprint, grocery lists, tissues. Patton popped his head out of the centre and blinked at me.

I approached cautiously. He didn't bother to move while I scanned the pile for my registration paper. I didn't see it anywhere on the top of the pile.

I started to shuffle some papers around, and Patton sat up, watching my movements with interest. I think he was too lazy to be territorial about his space.

I found a notice for jury duty for Noah, dated 1989. There was a selection of birthday cards, most of them from Grace, which spanned the last 40 years.

There it was. I picked it up and carefully wiped a glob of drool off the corner with my shirt. I made to stand, and the paper I had just uncovered caught my eye.

It was an unopened envelope. Addressed to 2B.

I was 2B.

I picked it up just as Noah's voice bellowed from near the front door. "Jordan! Get a move on!"

I hurried down the hall and out the door with the envelope tucked into my back pocket.

I sat at the back of the city bus. The seats around me were filled with kids my age; some excited, some nervous, all about to take the next step of their lives. There were a few adults that stood surrounded by the chaos and smiled to themselves, reliving memories of their first months away from home, out in the world. One by one they pulled the cord and got off the bus. With each exit, the noise of youth and passion and excitement grew until it filled the whole bus.

I sat at the back of the bus, and read.

Dear Whoever-You-Are,

Just wanted to leave you a note before I go. Hope you enjoy the place. The neighbours keep to themselves, so you won't be bothered much. I lived in 2B for three years, and I didn't have many issues.

There was a slight concern with dampness in the kitchen awhile ago. Mr. Foster had some people come in and fix it. They said as long as you don't steam the place up too much, it won't be a problem.

I'll leave this message with Mr. Foster, to give to you. Hopefully he doesn't forget.

Finally, I'd made a deal with our Postal Service guy to deliver all the mail in our complex to your unit. He asked me to last year, says he does it at a few places and it saves about a half-hour on his run. Guess he wanted a longer lunch break. It didn't matter to me, so I agreed. If you don't want to, just leave him a note on the chair, he'll stop.

Enjoy Stony Creek Estates!

Norman Crawley (previously 2B)

PS. I hope you like opera.

I sat there considering my options, surrounded by the anticipated life.

By the time the bus had arrived on campus, I'd made my decision. There would be no note placed on the white plastic chair.

Why mess with a good thing?

I came off the bus into the morning light. The Student Centre rose in front of me, all glass and metal, polished and bright, reflecting our futures.

I walked to the front door and stepped through.

The first thing I noticed was the people.

Acknowledgements

I would like to thank Kari and Matt, who were there when this idea was born, my parents, Ron and Heike, for serving as my toughest critics and my biggest fans as the story grew, and especially my wife, Krista, for her unswerving support of my decision to sit down and try to fashion these words into a book. Thank you.

About the Author

Jason Vikse is a Canadian author and confirmed bibliophile. After years of working in bookstores and libraries he finally decided to try his hand at the creative process of writing. Whether it works out or not is up to you. He currently lives in Melbourne with his wife, Krista, where he spends his free time on the stage as a theatrical actor and director. This is his first book.

Made in the USA
Lexington, KY
11 August 2012